Our Christmas Story

Our Christmas Story

by Ruth Bell Graham

**as told to
Elizabeth Sherrill**

Illustrations by David Koechel

**world wide
publications**

1303 Hennepin Avenue, Minneapolis, Minnesota 55403

ACKNOWLEDGEMENTS

Scripture quotations taken from The Living Bible, copyright © 197
by Tyndale House Publishers, Wheaton, Illinois 60187.
Used by permission.

ISBN 0-89066-005-0

Library of Congress Catalog Number 73-84958.

Printed in the U.S.A.

Foreword

When it was suggested that Ruth tell the Christmas story for children everywhere, we were delighted. But we had to warn the publisher that "our" Christmas story would be different from the traditional manger scene that spells Christmas for many people.

Of course, the manger scene is an important part of Christmas in our home — the joyous and beloved climax to the story. But it is only a part of the story. For Christmas does not begin in the stable of Bethlehem. It does not begin in the Gospel of Luke, but in the Book of Genesis.

Visitors to our home at Christmas are sometimes startled when I read the tragic story from the Old Testament before an evening of carols.

"Aren't these grim thoughts for this happy time of year?" they ask. "The season of Jesus's birth is no time to talk of death. What do Adam and Eve have to do with Christmas?"

To which we answer: Everything. Without the story of sin in the Old Testament, what can the good news of the New Testament say? Without sin, we have no need of a Savior. We cannot separate our joy at Christ's coming from our desperate need for Him. Unless we have witnessed the tragedy of man's separation from God through the millennia before Bethlehem, then the birth of a baby in a stable is just that for us, no more.

Nor can we separate His birth from the work He came to earth to do. Without His death, His birth has no meaning. The birth without the Cross is a gift half-given. Many would rather not think of the Cross at Christmastime. They take the angels' song, but reject all that it implies. In doing this, they rob themselves of the full joy of Christmas.

Children are more realistic than adults. They have no trouble in grasping the real meaning of good and evil in a story. In this respect, we need to be more like children. When we see Christmas not as a sentimental, isolated event, but as the focal point in human history, it becomes a day of rejoicing indeed.

Here, of course, that history must be simplified and abbreviated. No one is more aware than Ruth of what her book leaves out and what it does not say. It is not a theological treatise, but a book for children. Ruth has tried to hint at the riches of the Bible, not to provide an inventory of them. Her hope is that this approach to Christmas will lead the readers of this book to the Bible itself for the full story in all its wonder.

Ruth and I believe that it has never been more important than it is today for children to read and love the Bible. In this age of "go with the crowd," boys and girls can take courage from its lonely giants — men like Noah and Moses — who, as Ruth expresses it, closed their ears to the many in order to listen to the One.

If this little book helps children to see in the whole Bible the glorious meaning of Christ's coming, Ruth's prayers — and mine — for it will be abundantly answered.

Contents

Christmas at Our House

*My mother always
served oyster stew for
Christmas breakfast
when I was a girl
in China. It was a
family custom.*

Christmas at Our House

*D*o you ever have oysters for breakfast?

We do, once a year, on Christmas morning.

Perhaps you wonder why we have them then. When I go to the grocery store the day before Christmas and ask for oysters, I like to tell the man when I'm going to serve them.

"Oysters for breakfast!" he says, and he is very puzzled. Then I explain that my mother always served oyster stew for Christmas breakfast when I was a girl in China. It was a family custom. And when my father, who is a doctor, decided that it was time to bring his family back to America we brought back the custom of oysters for Christmas breakfast, too.

Let's pretend that you've come to visit us on Christmas. There's a special reason why it has to be Christmas, of all the days in the year. This is the day when, after all the presents are opened, we sit in front of the fire and hear the Christmas story from the Bible. I want you to pretend that you're hearing it with us because, later, I want to ask you a question about it.

Of course, your own parents can't really spare you for Christmas. Christmas is one of those days when parents want their families at home. This will be just a pretend visit — and that will have one advantage: you'll only have to eat pretend oysters.

I'll tell you about our house so that you can imagine you are here. In the first place, there are our dogs. One is a Great Pyrenees. His name is Belshazzar because in Old Testament times there was a king named Belshazzar who gave a great feast for a thousand lords, and every time we see Belshazzar eat we feel as though we're feeding a thousand lords, too. He's so big you can ride on his back. Our children do, so there's no reason why you can't.*

Our house will make you think of a pioneer's cabin off in the woods. We asked the men who built it to leave the logs showing and the walls rough, like those of an old-fashioned log cabin. It's just the place to run and make things and play with the dogs and not worry

*Belshazzar is no longer with us but has been replaced by other pets.

14

about the furniture.

And if you like to do things with people your own age, I'm sure you'll like it up here. We have five children of our own and at Christmastime there is always a bunch of cousins, too. Our own children are:

Gigi (she's the oldest, and her real name isn't Gigi — it's Virginia)

Ann (who has such a short name we couldn't make it any shorter)

Bunny (Bunny's real name is Ruth, like mine)

Franklin (whose real name is Franklin)

Ned ("Ned" is short — very short — for Nelson Edman)

So you'll be certain to find someone your own age to do things with, up here.**

When I say "up here," I mean up on a mountain. Our house is almost at the top, with a very steep road leading up to it. There are lots of places to explore. You might try the cave down the hill, or the orchard behind the house where the bears come. Don't worry about the bears; they are sleeping at Christmastime. Besides, the dogs are bound to be tagging along behind you, and they're so big they'd give any bear quite a scare.

But now let's say that it's Christmas morning. The tree is over there by the window, with the presents

*The Graham children are grown up now and have their own little families.

beneath it and its branches loaded down with warm-colored lights, candy canes, ornaments, and the smallest gifts. And here in front of the enormous fireplace — big enough to stand up in, when there's no fire — are the stockings, one for every child and cousin and, of course, one for you. The presents have to wait until after breakfast, but the stockings are for now.

After the stockings comes breakfast, and you know what is on the table today, don't you? Oysters, floating in a big, steaming stew. (Want to know a secret? Personally, I don't like oysters for breakfast. I never did, not even when I was a girl, about your age, back in China. But the stew part is fine.)

Our children think breakfast takes forever on Christmas morning. Never do the grown-ups eat so much. They sit around and drink cup after cup of coffee, and they lean back and talk about how long it's been since they were all together, and they even waste precious minutes looking out over the valley and saying what a lovely day it is. But then comes the wonderful moment when finally they're through, and they get up, scraping their chairs on the floor, and everyone goes back into the living room to open the presents.

It takes a long time because everyone wants to see what everyone else has received. But finally the very last package is opened. The floor is a heap of paper

16

and ribbons and the grown-ups are saying, as they did last year, that there's really too much and that next year they will have to buy fewer presents.

And now comes the moment that's really Christmas. The fire is snapping. Christmas music is playing softly on the record player. Everyone makes himself comfortable, some on the floor, some in chairs, some on the window seat. It's time for the Christmas story. Father opens the Bible to the second chapter of the Book of Luke. When he begins to read the room is suddenly still with a special stillness that it has only at this time on Christmas morning. We are very quiet as we listen again to the wonderful story:

About this time Caesar Augustus, the Roman Emperor, decreed that a census should be taken throughout the nation....Everyone was required to return to his ancestral home for this registration. And because Joseph was a member of the royal line, he had to go to Bethlehem in Judea, King David's ancient home — journeying there from the Galilean village of Nazareth. He took with him Mary, his fiancee, who was obviously expecting a child by this time. And while they were there, the time came for her baby to be born; and she gave birth to her first child, a son. She wrapped him in a blanket and laid him in a manger, because there

was no room for them in the village inn. That night
some shepherds were in the fields outside the village,
guarding their flocks of sheep. Suddenly an angel
appeared among them,..."Don't be afraid!" he said.
"I bring you the most joyful news ever announced,
and it is for everyone! The Savior — yes, the Messiah,
the Lord — has been born tonight in Bethlehem!"

The fire is burning low. The cat is purring. Outside, perhaps it has begun to snow. The special quiet that the Christmas story brings has filled the whole room.

Now here is the question I wanted to ask you: Is this the very beginning of the Christmas story? Or does it sound as though we had started right in the middle of it? The angel called this Baby a Savior — someone who saves. If you fell through the ice when you were skating and a man rushed up to pull you from the water, that man would be your savior. But if this Baby was a Savior, what was he to save us from? It sounds as if there were a lot more to the story.

What is the whole Christmas story? It's really much too long to tell now, when we have all the ribbons and boxes to pick up and Christmas dinner to fix. Besides, the best stories aren't told all at once. They're told little by little, as we dry the dishes or get ready for bed. Bedtime is really the best time for storytelling.

There's only one thing to do. We'll just have to pretend that you're spending the whole week with us. Then every night, at bedtime, I can tell you a little more of the Christmas story, starting from the very beginning.

We'll imagine you are sleeping in the guest room. There's the biggest bed in there you ever saw — an old-fashioned press bed, higher than your head. In fact, another bed fits underneath it. That other bed is called a trundle bed because it "trundles" out from under the big one. Maybe you'd rather sleep in the trundle bed — if anyone ever fell out of the high one he'd hit awfully hard!

When story time comes each evening, we'll gather all the children that are around and we'll pile onto the bed with you and listen. I've told them the story dozens of times, but they never get tired of hearing it.

In the Beginning

In the Beginning

If the Book of Luke gives us only part of the Christmas story, where is the rest of it?

To find the beginning of the story, we have to go back a long way. The first Christmas when Jesus was born in Bethlehem was almost two thousand years ago, but we have to go back farther than that. We have to go back before Mary and Joseph themselves were born. Back before there was any town of Bethlehem. Before there were any towns at all. Even before there were any people on the earth. In fact, so far back that there was no earth.

There were no stars then either. No sun, no sky, no rain. In those days — except that there were no

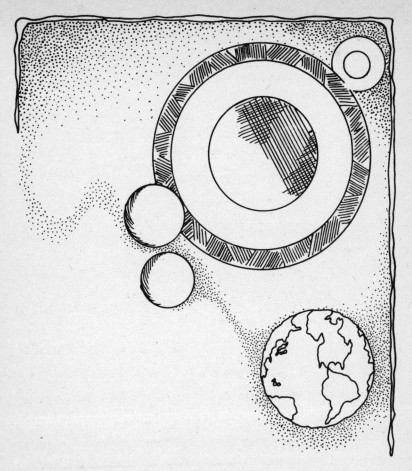

At first the universe was dark, so God made the burning stars — our sun among them — for light. He made our earth and then He filled it with wonders.

days — space was empty. In all the universe, there was only God Himself — and the angels.

The Christmas story goes back that far.

In that long ago, unimaginable time, God began to make things. He made things because He was God, and God loves to make things.

At first the universe was dark, so God made the burning stars — our sun among them — for light. He made our earth and then He filled it with wonders. He put deep oceans and high mountains on it. In the oceans He put octopuses and giant fish and creatures so tiny that only He could see them. On the mountains He put goats, and He made them wonderful climbers. In the valleys He put all sorts of animals — caterpillars and parrots and rhinoceroses. And of course, He made oysters! He made billions and trillions of creatures and not one was exactly like another.

God loved the things He had made. He loved His raindrops and His octopuses and His daylight. But He had no children to share them with Him. In all the earth, there was no one like Himself, no one to say, "How beautiful it is!" And no one to enjoy it with Him.

In the whole earth, no one to have a conversation with! God talked to His creation, of course. He talked to His flowers with His warm sunshine and His cool rain. In every little fish egg He put a message, telling that egg how to grow into a fish instead of a rhinoceros. And all of His creatures obeyed Him, but not one of them answered Him.

To have a companion on earth, God needed someone like Himself. So He made one more creature. He made our kind of creature and He made it in His own image. That is, He copied us after Himself.

He made two of us, a man and a woman. The man's name was Adam and the woman's name was Eve. As soon as He had made them, God loved them more than all the other creatures He had made. He wanted to shower them with gifts. He gave them all His cows and His fish and His bees — yes, and His oysters, too. Every animal on the whole earth and in all the oceans he gave to Adam and Eve. He gave them all His trees and plants. From the tallest date palm to the flattest mushroom, they were all for Adam and Eve.

Then He found the most beautiful spot on earth for them to live in. It was named Eden and it was so beautiful it was called a garden. In the Garden of Eden God put everything that Adam and Eve needed to make them happy. There were rivers of clear water to drink, fruit to eat, vines to swing on, flowers to smell.

They didn't need spears, or any kind of weapon,

He gave them all His trees
and plants. From the tallest
date palm to the flattest
mushroom, they were all for
Adam and Eve.

because they had no enemies. There were no wild animals in those days either. Lions and bears and hyenas came when Adam called them and lay down on the ground to be played with, because they knew they belonged to him. Adam loved the animals and they loved him.

Adam and Eve didn't need a house to live in or warm clothes to wear because it was never cold in Eden, and God kept the wind and the rain off of them. They didn't need a stove or a refrigerator or even pans to cook with, since all the food they wanted grew on the trees for them. And they certainly didn't need money, since God had already given them everything.

God watched the two people He had made, and He loved them. He was delighted when Eve picked the flowers and gave them pretty names and put them in her hair. "She loves My flowers!" God thought. He liked to see Adam stroke the lions and the buffaloes and call them wonderful and handsome and marvelous. Best of all, He liked to hear Adam and Eve say, "All these things were made by God."

For work, God gave them the care of His beautiful garden. Adam and Eve loved their work. All morning they pruned the trees and dug the earth until it was soft around the flowers. Then, when their work was finished, they would run with the antelope, swim with

God watched the two people He had made,
and He loved them. He was delighted
when Eve picked the flowers and gave them
pretty names and put them in her hair.

the otter, sing with the oriole. Best of all, they would wait for the moment of God's visit.

For God loved Adam and Eve so much that every evening, at the close of the long, happy day, He came into the garden and talked with them. And then — new joy on earth! — the man and the woman answered Him. It was the moment God had waited for since He had created the world.

"At last," He thought, "I have My children with whom I can share the joy and the glory of My creation."

The Testing Tree

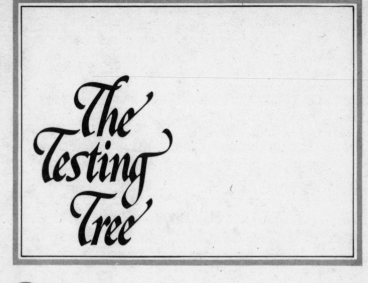

The Testing Tree

So far, this has been a happy story because it has been about God's plan for His world — and for us. God's plan was for us to live always in perfect fellowship with Him. In His plan, there was no sickness, no hunger, no war, no unhappiness. We were to be His companions, to live closer to Him than His other creatures.

But wait. Are we living the happy life God planned? Has anyone you know ever been sick? Do people fight wars? Do you ever quarrel with your brothers and sisters? Is there unhappiness in the world? Something must have gone wrong with God's plan.

Something did go wrong, and the something was

this: the people whom God had made did not follow His plan.

But, you say, He was God! Why didn't He *make* them follow it?

But there, you see, was the difference between the animals God had made and these new creatures called humans. Animals *must* follow God's plan for them; they have no choice. A caterpillar does not say to himself, "Let's see, shall I spin myself a cocoon and turn into a butterfly, or is it more fun just to be a caterpillar?" He spins a cocoon because he cannot help it.

But from human beings, God wanted something more than blind, unthinking obedience. He wanted Adam and Eve to follow His plan not because they had to, but because they wanted to. He wanted them to join Him willingly, eagerly in fellowship rather than mechanical agreement. He wanted them to be people rather than robots. And so, to man alone, God gave the power of choice.

It was a bold experiment, because there was the terrible possibility that this new creature might choose *not* to follow God's plan. That was the risk God took when He made Adam and Eve. But, in His love God took that risk.

In the very center of the Garden of Eden was a tall and beautiful tree on which grew a strange and lovely

In the very center of the Garden of Eden was a tall and beautiful tree on which grew a strange and lovely fruit.

fruit. But beautiful though it was, this tree was forbidden to Adam and Eve.

"If you eat its fruit, you will be doomed to die," God had said.

This was the testing tree, to see whether Adam and Eve would choose to follow God's plan. "Surely," thought God, "it is an easy test, when there are hundreds of trees in the garden whose fruit they may eat. After all I have done for them, surely they will do this much for Me."

Here is where sorrow enters the story. For Adam and Eve, instead of listening to God who had made them, listened to the words of someone who hated them.

One day a snake who lived in the garden came up to Eve.

"Really?" asked the snake in his skeptical voice. *"None of the fruit in the garden? God says you mustn't eat any of it?"*

"Of course we may eat it," said Eve. *"It's only the fruit from the tree at the center of the garden that we are not to eat. God says we mustn't eat it or even touch it, or we will die."*

The snake laughed a secret laugh. "Are you sure He said that?" he hissed. *"You'll not die! God knows very well that the instant you eat it you will become like Him, for your eyes will be opened — you will be able to tell good from evil!* It will make you wise! As wise as God! Eat it," he whispered, "and you will know everything that He knows!"

Now this snake, as you have already guessed, was no ordinary animal. This was Satan himself. Once, long, long before, Satan had been an angel living with God in heaven. But he was so proud of living with God that he began to imagine he was just as good as God — maybe even better! And so God had to send him away. Like a bolt of lightning Satan fell from heaven. Now, in Adam and Eve, he saw a way to get even, a way to spoil God's plan.

To Eve, the snake's words sounded wonderful. To be wise as God! She shut her mind to what God had said about the tree. In fact, she turned her back on God and His plan. She was full of her own plans now.

She ran to the center of the garden and looked up into the branches of the testing tree. There, just above her, ripe and tempting, hung the fruit. She picked one. For a moment she wondered if it would really kill her. She took a tiny bite of it and waited. Nothing happened. She felt as strong as ever and the fruit was so good! She ate it all and then she picked a piece for Adam and took it to him. And Adam ate it.

It was the first evil thing that ever happened on this earth.

Good-bye to the Garden

Good-bye to the Garden

There is a special word for the evil thing that Adam and Eve did. The word is "sin." To sin means to disobey God, to fall short of His goodness. When Adam and Eve ate the fruit that God had told them not to eat, they committed the first sin, so it is sometimes called "the original sin."

At first, Adam and Eve couldn't see that their sin had hurt them at all. They waited, a bit afraid, for God had said, "You will be doomed to die" — but, after all, they were still alive. So they decided that God had not really meant it.

But Adam and Eve did not understand the kind of death God was talking about. That death was three-fold. One part of it had happened instantly — their wonderful fellowship with God had already ended. Part of it had just begun — now everything in the world was under a death sentence. All plants and animals and Adam and Eve themselves would grow old and die. Finally, there was the death of being forever separated from God. But already God was planning a way by which His wayward children could return to Him. This dreadful eternal death would be only for those who refused to follow God's way.

This is what God had warned Adam and Eve about. He had said, "If you choose not to obey Me, then you will be cutting yourself off from Me, and this death will follow." Though Adam and Eve did not know it, it had already begun.

They had scarcely swallowed the fruit when a feeling came over them that they had never felt before. The feeling was shame!

At that moment, they heard God's voice in the garden. He had come for His evening visit and He was calling them.

"Adam! Eve!"

Adam and Eve looked at each other in terror. Always before they had run to meet Him, for this was the best moment of the day. But now they were afraid. For the first time, they did not want to be near

God. They wanted to run far away from Him, to put their fingers in their ears, to pretend they didn't hear.

And so they tried to hide from God. They ran behind some trees and waited, hoping that He would go away.

But God waited for these two children of His. When they did not come, He called to Adam, "Where are you?"

And Adam came out from behind the trees. He was trembling all over, and he said to God, *"I heard you coming and didn't want you to see me naked."*

Now this was not the truth. The real reason Adam hid was that he had disobeyed God and was afraid he'd be punished. But he still hoped God wouldn't find out about the fruit from the testing tree. So he lied to God.

God's voice was sorrowful and He said, *"Who told you you were naked? Have you eaten fruit from the tree I warned you about?"*

Now Adam saw that there was no use in trying to deceive God. But he still thought perhaps God would not be angry at him if he could blame somebody else. So he pointed to Eve and said, *"It was the woman you gave me who brought me some, and I ate it."*

Then God turned to Eve and when He spoke His voice was stern. "Eve," He said, *"How could you do such a thing?"*

No matter how hard Adam worked, the fruit and grain that he grew did not taste as good as the fruit in the Garden of Eden. Thorns and thistles grew up out of the ground and choked what he planted. When he tried to pull these weeds up, they scratched his hands.

Now Eve was frightened and she looked around for someone to blame. "The snake did it!" she said. "He talked me into it! It was his fault."

But God was not impressed by excuses. All three had done wrong. All three had to take the consequences.

God turned first to the snake. *"You shall grovel in the dust as long as you live, crawling along on your belly."* And ever since, snakes have squirmed along the ground.

As for Adam and Eve, they had shut themselves away from the happy life God had planned for them in the Garden of Eden. They were driven into the windy, cold, rainy world outside. Instead of simply reaching up into the trees for their dinner, they had to plant seeds and pull weeds and raise their own food.

And no matter how hard Adam worked, the fruit and grain that he grew did not taste as good as the fruit in the Garden of Eden. Thorns and thistles grew up out of the ground and choked what he planted. When he tried to pull these weeds up, they scratched his hands. Adam wondered where they came from; he had never seen such things in the garden God had planted.

But worst of all, Adam and Eve had separated themselves from God. They could no longer be the very thing they had been created to be in the first place — God's companions on the earth. The warm and constant fellowship with God was broken. They had stepped outside His plan and now they were homeless.

The Man Who Listened

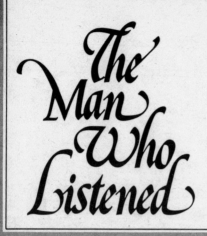

The Man Who Listened

The first sin brought unhappiness to Adam and Eve. But the unhappiness it brought them was nothing compared to the grief it brought God. Here were the creatures He had chosen out of all the universe to be His companions — and they had left Him.

He was lonely again, but now His loneliness was worse than before, because He had had children and then lost them. God, you see, still loved these people He had made. God does not change. No matter how badly they had behaved, they were still His dearest creation.

And so, when they left the Garden, He went with them — with Adam and Eve and their children and their children's children's children — calling them, warning them of danger, trying to teach them. But they wouldn't listen, these children of Adam. Just as Adam and Eve had disobeyed God, so did the people who came after them. Year by year they drifted farther away from God's plan.

Adam and Eve had two sons, Abel and Cain. When they grew up, Cain killed his brother, and that was the first murder. Adam and Eve had more children, and those children had children until there were many people in the world — and most of them were like Cain.

Instead of living together peacefully, they quarreled with each other. The more people a soldier killed in a war, the greater a hero he was. Next to wars, the children of Adam liked noisy pleasures best. In their so-called fun they screamed and shouted and spilled their food like spoiled children, and bragged about how many people they would kill in the next war.

In all the noisy confusion no one heard God calling. No one heard Him say, over and over, that this was not what He had made them for.

At least, very few people heard Him. In every generation there were always one or two who tried hard to shut out the din around them so that they could hear what God was saying.

One of these people was a man called Noah. Noah didn't go to war to kill his neighbors, and he didn't go to the noisy parties. He lived quietly with his wife and three sons, listening all the time for God's message.

Now it happened that God had a very important message for Noah. The Bible tells us:

When the Lord God saw the extent of human wickedness, and that the trend and direction of men's lives were only towards evil, he was sorry he had made them. It broke his heart.

So God decided to wash the whole earth clean with a great rain. But Noah was a good man, and God told him about the flood that was coming. He told Noah to build an ark — a large boat with a house on its deck — big enough to hold his family and some of every kind of animal in the world.

God told Noah exactly how to build it, how long it should be, and how high. *"Construct decks and stalls throughout the ship,"* He said. *"Make three decks inside the boat — a bottom, middle, and upper deck."* He told Noah to put one door and one window in the ark.

Of course, when Noah's loud-mouthed neighbors, who were sitting around wondering what new trouble they could stir up, heard all the hammering at Noah's house, they rushed over to see what old Noah was up to.

When the last chipmunk and caterpillar
were in the ark God Himself shut them in.

"He's always got some crazy notion," one man shouted.

"Thinks he hears 'God' talking!" shrieked another. "As if there was any such thing as 'God'!"

When they got there and found Noah building a huge boat on dry land, miles and miles from the ocean, they laughed until the tears rolled down their cheeks.

Noah didn't mind. He was used to standing alone and he was used to being laughed at. He didn't care what people thought, so long as he knew what God thought. Now the boat was almost ready. Noah and his three sons led the animals into the ark and his wife and his sons' wives carried in the last of the food: seed for the birds, grain for the cattle and horses, dried fruit for themselves — every kind of food there was, enough to last for a long, long time. When the last chipmunk and caterpillar were in the ark God Himself shut them in. At that, seeing them all aboard a boat on dry land, Noah's noisy neighbors laughed louder than ever.

And while they were laughing, it began to rain.

Day and night, the storm continued. In the pale light of their oil lamps, Noah and his family sat and listened to the terrible rain pounding on the roof. After many days they felt the ark gently rocking, and they knew it was floating on the water.

For forty nights the rain poured down. When at last it stopped and Noah opened the window to look out, there was only water, stretching as far as his eyes could see. Not even the tops of the mountains showed above the water. But perhaps, thought Noah, there is dry land farther ahead, out of sight, And so, as the Bible tells us:

...He sent out a dove to see if it could find dry ground, but the dove found no place to light, and returned to Noah, for the water was still too high. So Noah held out his hand and drew the dove back into the boat.
Noah waited a week.
...Noah released the dove again, and this time, towards evening, the bird returned to him with an olive leaf in her beak.

So Noah knew that the waters were slowly going down and that somewhere the top of a tree had appeared. But it was a whole year from the time the rain began until the earth was dry enough to walk on again. Then out of the ark they ran, Noah and his family and all the animals that had been cooped up so long, to stretch their legs on the good earth again. They wanted to skip and run and shout for joy, they were

...Noah released the dove
again, and this time, towards
evening, the bird returned
to him with an olive leaf
in her beak.

so glad to get out of the crowded boat. But before he did anything else, Noah built an altar to God, and offered Him a solemn prayer of thanks.

And God looked down on His world, and He saw that of all His people only Noah and his family were left. "But now," thought God, "these people will be different. They have seen what happens when men do not listen to Me. Noah's children will not forget Me."

And at first, they didn't forget. Noah's sons remembered the great Flood and told their sons about it. The sons' sons heard about it, but it seemed like a long time ago. So after a while people began to forget why their family had lived through the Flood. They forgot how important it was to listen to God, and they began to do whatever they wanted to instead. Once more people decided not to follow God's plan.

It was God's plan for all of Noah's children to have enough to eat. But they didn't follow God's plan. If a man was strong, he would take all the wheat from his neighbor's fields and all the fruit from his trees, and lock them up in his own storehouse. If other people starved, why should he care?

When he became very rich the strong man called himself a ruler and then he not only took the wheat and fruit that other people had raised, but whole cities that other people had built, to get the gold that was

They invented many little gods to suit their own plans: a god to help them win wars, a god to make it rain, a god to chase wolves away.

in them. He even took the people who lived in the cities and made them his slaves. Then while his slaves struggled with heavy stones to build a storehouse for his stolen gold, the ruler sat back and decided what city he would take next to get more gold and more slaves.

There was little kindness in the world that Noah's children built. Most men did not care how unhappy other people were, so long as they themselves were getting rich.

As for loving God, by this time most people had forgotten God and His plan altogether. They invented many little gods to suit their own plans: a god to help them win wars, a god to make it rain, a god to chase wolves away.

They even imagined what these gods looked like. One god, they thought, was a bull with wings, another had the body of a cat and the face of a man, another one was supposed to be in the shape of a snake.

And God, watching His people, saw that they were getting more confused all the time. "There is only one God!" He kept trying to tell them. "I am not shaped like a bull or a cat or a snake! You can't see Me with your eyes; you must see Me with your heart. Love Me and you will see Me! Love anyone at all and you will catch a glimpse of me!"

It was no use. Most people were not listening any

more. They had shut their ears to Him for so long
that they did not even recognize God's voice.

The Chosen People

The Chosen People

But, as always, a few men did listen. One of these men was Abraham. Abraham lived in a rich and beautiful city called Haran. But one day he heard God's voice say:

Leave your own country behind you, and your own people, and go to the land I will guide you to.

If you do, I will cause you to become the father of a great nation...and the entire world will be blessed because of you.

Abraham was seventy-five years old when he heard these words but, hard as it was to leave his home, he obeyed God, left Haran, and went into the new land.

For many years Abraham and then his sons and his

grandsons were wandering herdsmen in this new land. And God repeated His promise to Abraham's grandson, Jacob.

And God said to him, "You shall no longer be called Jacob, but Israel. I am God Almighty," the Lord said to him..."a great nation, yes, many nations, many kings shall be among your descendants....And I will pass on to you the land I gave to Abraham and... I will give it to you and to your descendants."

But when Jacob (or Israel) was an old man, there was a great famine in this land, and to find food Israel and his children had to leave and go to a country called Egypt. There they were eventually made slaves. For hundreds of years they worked for the Egyptians. It seemed almost as if God had forgotten His promise that He would make them a great nation. But God never forgets.

Egypt in those days was the richest country in the world: the Pharaoh had more slaves and more gold and more storehouses than any other king. The Pharaoh and all the other Egyptians believed in many different gods and built huge temples for them, thinking that the more temples a god had the more pleased he would be and the more favors he would do for Egypt. But since none of their gods really existed, the great temples were wasted.

To find food Israel and
his children had to leave and
go to a country called Egypt.
There they were eventually
made slaves. For hundreds of
years they worked for
the Egyptians.

The Egyptians forced their slaves to build their temples for them, and as the years went by many of the Israelites forgot God and worshiped the false gods of Egypt. Perhaps a few were true to the one God; we do not know. But they dared not worship Him openly. All day they slaved in the mud pits, making bricks for the temples of the Egyptians. But at night, while the Egyptians were chanting and singing in the great temples, perhaps these few went back to the hovels where they lived, locked their doors, and prayed in whispers to the one true God.

And God heard their prayers. He hears whispers just as clearly as shouts, and He likes hovels as well as palaces.

God needed these humble slaves. Why did He need them? He needed them to entrust with the gift that He was preparing for all mankind. God was getting ready for Christmas, and the gift He was giving the world was so priceless and so rare that He could not place it in unworthy hands.

You see, God had thought of a way to bring His children back to Him — the children He had lost — and this way was Christmas.

It seems strange that He still wanted them back, these people who had disappointed Him so often. They had brought Him little but sorrow ever since

He had created them. He had given them the power
to choose, and they had chosen to disobey Him.
He had created them to be His friends, and they spent
most of their time fighting each other. He had talked
with them, and they had turned away. He ought to
have been thoroughly tired of them.

But He wasn't. God's patience does not wear out,
as man's does. It did not matter what men did or
how long they stayed away from Him, He still longed
for them as a father longs for a child who has run away.

But God had seen that, by themselves, they would
never find their way back to Him. It didn't matter
whether He started with Adam or Noah, with bad
men or good men; sooner or later people wandered
outside His plan and were hopelessly separated
from Him.

Have you ever watched a fly trying to go straight
through a closed window? It flies at the glass again
and again, trying to get into the clear air beyond.
The fly doesn't know — but you know — that he
will never get past that glass unless you take pity
on him and open the window.

That must have been how God felt as He watched
men flying at the wall they had built between themselves and Him. "They're never going to get past that
wall," God must have said, "unless I open a way for

them. They are separated from Me, and this separation is death.

"But what if I were to take away this death that follows sin? What if I sent my Son to take this death for men, so that they would not have to die?"

If it seems to be a cruel answer, we must remember that sin is cruel, that what it does to men is cruel, and that to save us from this death, God had to give the very life of His Son. For Jesus is the way that God opened to us, the way back to fellowship with Him.

But how could the Son of God die? God's Son was One with God Himself. He was not a man. He was Spirit. Like God's, His life had no beginning. How could His life end when it had never begun?

To die, the Son of God would have to be born. This is the gift God was planning. He was going to send His Son to earth as a human baby. He would be born, just as you were, a tiny infant too weak to lift up its head. He would have to learn all the things other babies learn: how to crawl, how to stand, how to run. Later He would be a boy, no faster runner than any other boy in town. He would live in His family's house, help around the home, and obey His parents and teachers.

And then, when He was a man, He would bring men back to the God they had forgotten. He would

tell them why God had made them and put them
on this earth. He would tell them:

The Lord our God is the one and only God. And you
must love Him with all your heart and soul and mind
and strength...and...you must love others as much
as yourself.

He would show them, too, as well as tell them.
In His own life they could see what God meant by
"love." He would feed the hungry and heal the sick
and make the blind see.

And finally He would show them the greatest love
of all: He would die for them, and after that the way
would be opened for all who would to return to God.

After that no matter how a person sinned, no matter
how far from God's plan he wandered, there would
still be this way back. For love like this would be
stronger than sin — stronger than death itself.

This was the gift God was preparing, and this was
why He needed the children of Israel. These humble
slaves were to make a home on earth for His Son.
"There shall come a Star out of Jacob," He said,
"and a Sceptre shall rise out of Israel." Already God
saw the star over Bethlehem and Jesus as Lord of
all mankind.

There was a man in Egypt named Moses. He was
an Israelite by birth, but he had been adopted as a

baby by Pharaoh's daughter and raised as an Egyptian Prince. The Bible tells us he *"chose to share ill-treatment with God's people instead of enjoying the pleasures of sin for a little while."* He was God's man for the tremendous task that lay ahead.

"Come," said God to Moses. "Now I am going to send you to Pharaoh, to demand that he let you lead my people out of Egypt."

Moses knew that Pharaoh would be furious at such a suggestion. After all, why would a king want to let his valuable slaves go free? Then who would build his temples and do the unpleasant chores?

But Moses went to Pharaoh anyway and said, *"The God of Israel...says, 'Let my people go!'"*

As Moses had known he would, the king turned pale with anger. *"Who is the Lord,"* he asked haughtily, *"that I should listen to Him and let Israel go?"* And in his anger, he gave the children of Israel harder work to do.

Then God sent down plagues on Egypt. One of them was a plague of frogs. There were so many frogs that they covered the ground. They were everywhere the Egyptians stepped. They even hopped into their beds and jumped into the dough when the cooks tried to make bread.

The Egyptians prayed to all their gods and offered

God sent down plagues on Egypt. One of them was a plague of frogs. There were so many frogs that they covered the ground. They were everywhere the Egyptians stepped.

them fabulous gifts if they would only take the frogs away. The frogs only grew thicker. Then at last Pharaoh sent for Moses and said, not quite so haughtily, *"Plead with God to take the frogs away, and I will let the people go and sacrifice to Him."*

But Pharaoh was lying, for when God had taken the frogs away, he only laughed at Moses and would not keep his promise.

Then more plagues came to the Egyptians: lice, flies, boils, hail, locusts — and at last, the most dreadful of all — the death of the first born of men and animals. Now, in terror, the king begged Moses to take his people and leave Egypt at once.

The children of Israel grabbed their belongings and hurried out of Egypt as fast as they could, praising God for setting them free. But once more Pharaoh had tricked them. While they were resting from their fast march at the edge of a sea, they heard the sound of horses' hoofs in the distance. The sound came closer and now they could hear the chariot wheels, too. Pharaoh and his army were coming after them.

They were trapped, with the sea in front of them and Pharaoh closing in behind them!

The children of Israel cried to Moses, saying they should have stayed in Egypt.

"It would be better to be slaves to the Egyptians

than dead in the wilderness."

But Moses said to them, *"Don't be afraid. Just stand where you are and watch, and you will see the wonderful way the Lord will rescue you today. The Egyptians you are looking at — you will never see them again."*

And then with a mighty wind God blew back the water of the sea until there was a dry path through the middle of it and the children of Israel marched across to the other side on dry land. The chariots were close behind them. The Egyptians thundered into the dry path, too, their spears and arrows gleaming. But as the children of Israel reached the other side, the water closed in and Pharaoh's army was never seen again.

At last the children of Israel were free to worship the one true God. On a mountaintop there on the other side of the sea, God gave Moses the Ten Commandments and the other laws that His chosen people were to live by.

Then He led them into the land He had promised them. In those days it was called Canaan, but today it is known as the Holy Land because it was the home God chose for His Son.

Moses was an old man when the children of Israel reached Canaan, and he did not live to see them settled in their new land. But God spoke to His people through other men. One of them was a man named Isaiah and through Isaiah God told His people about the Savior who was coming:

The people who walk in darkness shall see a great Light — a Light that will shine on all those who live in the land of the shadow of death.

For unto us a Child is born; unto us a Son is given; and the government shall be upon his shoulders. These will be his royal titles: "Wonderful Counselor," "The Mighty God," "The Everlasting Father," "The Prince of Peace."

Where was this child to be born? Through a man named Micah, God gave the answer:

O Bethlehem...you are but a small Judean village, yet you will be the birthplace of my King who is alive from everlasting ages past.

God had chosen the people and the place. Now He had to choose the right time.

The Time Grows Short

The Time Grows Short

It had to be a very special time — the time when God's Son came into the world. It had to be a time when many people could understand one language. After His Son had done His great work of love, of course God would want people everywhere to know about it. He would want them to know that death was finished, that the long separation was over, that they could come back into that close fellowship with Him whenever they chose to, that sin could never again build an everlasting wall between them and God.

How was this wonderful news going to get to every person in the world? At first only the children of Israel would know about it.

But they would tell others. And those people would tell still more people, until the whole world knew what God had done. So, to pass the good news along from one person to the next, people had to be able to understand each other.

They had to be able to travel to distant places, too, so that the very farthest city on the other side of the mountains and the country beyond the sea would know. Therefore, at the time when God's Son was born, there had to be strong ships and wide roads.

God watched the world, waiting for His perfect time. Kings quarreled with each other, as they always had, and sometimes one of them was so strong that he conquered several countries and called himself an emperor. Then the emperor built roads to join his different countries and tried to make everyone speak his language.

But still it was not time. The roads were not good enough and the empires were not big enough. Hundreds of years went by, and still it was not time. It may seem to us like a long time to wait, but what to us are long, slow years, to God is only the blinking of an eye.

And then a city called Rome grew up, with the strongest army the world had ever seen. The Roman army conquered all the countries around Rome, and then the countries farther away, until Rome had conquered the whole world. (When the Romans said "the whole world," they didn't mean places like America and China and Australia because they didn't know about them. They meant only the part of the world that they knew.)

To make sure that all of these conquered people obey them, the Romans built roads to take their armies all over the known earth. They were very good roads — wide, stone roads. After all, the Romans had all the slaves in the world to lift the stones for them. They set other slaves to work building hundreds of speedy, sturdy ships. The roads and the ships were built for the army. But God, looking on, saw that they would be useful for something else.

One of the countries the Romans had conquered was Greece. Because the language of Greece was so beautiful and clear, many people spoke it. And God, listening, knew that Greek would be the perfect language for telling His good news.

If a man refused to obey the Roman laws, Roman soldiers marched down their broad highways and put him to death in a cruel way. The cruel way was "crucifixion," which means that the man was hung on a wooden cross until he died. God, watching, knew that the time was growing short. This was the way His Son must die.

God had one final choice to make. He had chosen the children of Israel to build a nation for His Son, and the town of Bethlehem as His birthplace. But the Baby still had no family to care for Him. God was His father, but the Baby needed a mother.

God searched among His people for a woman worthy to be the mother of His Son. Would she be a princess living in a palace; or a rich man's daughter who wore bright dresses and jewels and had maids to arrange her hair and rub it with sweet-smelling perfume? God did not choose one of these. He chose instead a modest young girl named Mary, who lived in the little hill town of Nazareth in Galilee. He sent His angel Gabriel to tell Mary that she had been chosen to be the mother of His Son.

...the angel told her..."Very soon now, you will... have a baby boy, and you are to name Him 'Jesus.' He shall be very great and shall be called the Son of God...And...His Kingdom shall never end!"

At first, Mary was so amazed that she could hardly speak. But she had always loved God and tried to obey Him. And so she said to the angel, "I am the Lord's servant, and I am willing to do whatever he wants. May everything you said come true."

She was going to marry a kind, strong man called

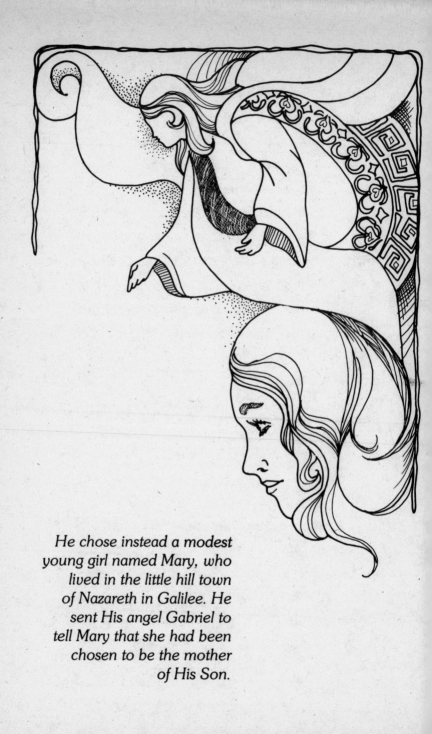

He chose instead a modest
young girl named Mary, who
lived in the little hill town
of Nazareth in Galilee. He
sent His angel Gabriel to
tell Mary that she had been
chosen to be the mother
of His Son.

Joseph. Long ago a man named Jeremiah had told the children of Israel that the Savior, when He came, would belong to the family of David, and both Mary and Joseph were members of that family, descended from the great King David. Joseph took good care of Mary as the time grew near for her Baby to be born.

But what about the words of Micah who had said that the Savior would be born in Bethlehem? Nazareth, where Joseph and Mary lived, was almost a hundred miles from Bethlehem by the twisting road, and in those days a hundred miles was a tremendous distance. But, as we shall see, Micah was right.

The emperor in Rome at that time was Caesar Augustus. That meant "Caesar the Splendid," and although the people didn't think he was splendid everybody in the world obeyed the emperor. But how many people was "everybody in the world"? Caesar didn't know.

So he decided to count them. Of course, he didn't want to count them just so that he could say, "Well, well. I am emperor of twenty million" (or however many it was). He wanted to know how many people he ruled so that he would know how much gold they could pay to him.

Each year every country in his empire had to send him a certain amount of gold as taxes. If it had no gold, the country had to send him its fattest sheep or a whole camel-train of its finest wheat. Of course, a large country had to give more to Caesar than a small country. So, in order to know how much each country should pay, Caesar had to count all the people in the world.

Now, in order to keep the different families and places in the huge empire straight, Caesar decided that everyone should go back to the town where his family had first lived, to be taxed there.

And when Caesar Augustus decided something, it was the law. All over the Roman world people had to go to their home towns and be counted for the tax. It might not be convenient to go. A farmer might be planting his wheat just then. It might not even be safe. There might be old people in a family, or a very young baby, or perhaps a sick person. But when Caesar said, "Go!" — people went.

Do you remember how it began, the story we heard on Christmas morning?

About this time Caesar Augustus, the Roman Emperor, decreed that a census should be taken throughout the nation....Everyone was required to return to his ancestral home for this registration. And because Joseph was a member of the royal line, he had to go to Bethlehem in Judea, King David's ancient

home — journeying there from the Galilean village
of Nazareth. He took with him Mary, his fiancée,
who was obviously expecting a child by this time.

Now is the time. Now is the very year and the very
day. This is the time for the Son of God to be born.

The First Christmas

The First Christmas

Of all the times in the world to live, imagine living
then! What if we had been alive on that very day!
What if we had lived not only at the very time but
had been in the very town where Jesus was born!

Nobody can choose when he will live. You and I
were born nearly two thousand years after that first
Christmas day, and had nothing to say about it. But
there's nothing to stop us from pretending — just as
we have been pretending that you are visiting us in our
home and sleeping on the trundle bed in our guest
room.

What if, instead of living in the twentieth century,
we had lived in Bethlehem just as the first century

began, and you had been our guest there? If you can imagine yourself up on the top of our mountain, you can imagine yourself over the ocean to Bethlehem. Then — but this is harder — you can imagine yourself back through time. Back through all those years. Back to the day when your bed was a blanket on the floor, when traveling by camel-back was the best way to get anywhere, and when Caesar Augustus was the ruler of the world.

Let's pretend that we lived in a little house in Bethlehem and you and your family were among the many descendants of David who had come to Bethlehem to be taxed. You might very well have stayed in our house. Bethlehem had only one small inn and that had been filled by the first travelers to arrive, so the rest had to find a place to sleep in the houses of strangers, or in stables or wherever there was room to lie down.

In that way, that first Christmas in Bethlehem would have been like our Christmas today. Our house would have been full of guests then, too, both grownups and children. But it wouldn't have been a happy get-together as it is today. It was no holiday then. Families were coming to Bethlehem to pay taxes to an emperor they hated. They came in fear and anger. They didn't know, you see, that Christmas was about to happen.

And of course we couldn't have offered you a
trundle bed to sleep in — in those days ordinary
people didn't have beds. Everybody carried his own
sleeping-blanket with him. During the day he wrapped
it about him as a cloak and at night he simply spread
it out on the floor and lay down on it. But at least
that made it easy to have guests. There was no counting
noses to make sure there were enough beds to go
around. A Bethlehem family could have as much
company as it had floor space.

There would have been no fireplace in our home
either; in Bethlehem people didn't use fireplaces.
And we probably wouldn't have eaten at a table.
We would have sat on mats on the floor and held
our meat and bread in our hands — and I'm sure
you children would have found that a more sensible
arrangement. Of course we wouldn't have had oyster
stew for breakfast, or at any other meal. The children
of Israel didn't eat oysters.

What would our names have been? Not Virginia
or Franklin or Nelson Edman, but Bunny and I could
still have been Ruth; Ann might have been Anna, and
we certainly could have had a dog named Belshazzar.

There wouldn't have been much time to play with
him, though, for we would all have been very busy.
I expect I would have spent most of the morning

turning the heavy grinding stone that women used in those days when they had to make their own flour and couldn't buy it in a sack at the grocery store.

In those days, too, all children were expected to help with the work. You boys would have gone with the men to the wheat fields outside the village. And the girls would have gone with me to fill our water jars at the public well down the street. We'd have balanced the big jars on our heads and stepped out cautiously into the narrow, crowded street.

Bethlehem was so crowded with travelers then that it must have been hard to move through the streets. Men tugged and shouted at heavy-laden donkeys, women carried tiny children, older children lugged bundles of food. The people in the streets looked cross and tired. Some of them were headed for the large house where the Roman soldiers were taking names for the tax rolls. Others had just arrived in Bethlehem and were peering anxiously into the crowded doorways, wondering where they would find a place to spend the night. All they needed was room enough to spread out their cloaks and a little water to wash the dust of travel from their feet, but even those simple things were hard to find then.

We would have edged along the crowds in the street, hoping no one would jostle us. Coming back would have been even slower, because the jars would be heavy. But when at last all the jars were filled, and the men's work in the fields was finished, I think I know where you would have gone. I think you would have headed for the gate where the north road came into Bethlehem. You would have climbed up onto the sun-warmed stone wall and sat down beside the other children and the old men to watch the latest strangers coming into town.

Here came a whole family: four children, the mother and father, the grandmother, and that very old woman on the donkey must be the great-grandmother. They looked tired as they trudged up this last hill. Probably they looked forward to a comfortable place to stay. You wished there were more room in our house.

Alone and in groups the people came, walking rapidly on this last bit of their journey, up the hill to Bethlehem. Some of them, the old men said, were coming from as far away as the town of Nazareth. You could hardly believe it. Almost a hundred miles! That meant three or four nights sleeping beside the road.

That man coming now, down in the valley, must be rich; he rode a camel! Not even his gold would buy him a room in Bethlehem tonight, you thought. You turned to the old man sitting beside you on the wall and, because old men knew everything, you asked him, "Why do all these people have to come to Bethlehem to be counted?"

The old man closed his eyes as if he were looking back over hundreds of years. "Their great-great-great-great-grandfathers once lived here," he said at last. "That makes this their home town, too, just as it's ours. And Caesar" — the old man leaned forward and spat on the road to show what he thought of Caesar — "Caesar doesn't care how far people have to travel if it makes his bookkeeping a little easier." The old man's eyes glared with anger.

The camel was lurching past you now. The rich rider's eyes were angry, too — angry and a little sad. It was the look in the eyes of all the travelers coming into Bethlehem. They didn't like having to make this trip, and they didn't like having to pay taxes to Rome. But what could they do? That was the way the world was. The strong took from the weak, the man with the sword made the laws, no one loved anyone but himself. It had always been that way, and always would be. There was nothing you could do to change it.

The afternoon sun was hot on your back. The wall was warm. For a minute, your eyes closed. When they opened, two people were coming along the dusty road down in the valley, a man walking and a woman riding

Two people were coming along the dusty road down in the valley, a man walking and a woman riding a donkey.

a donkey. But how slowly these two were coming. The woman had her hand on the man's shoulder and she seemed very weary. The man kept looking at her anxiously.

Two men walking rapidly with tall staffs passed the couple and the donkey, climbed the hill, and went in through the town gate. Now the man and woman had reached the hill and you could see the donkey was covered with dust, as if he had come a long way. Why were they stopping so often, now that their trip was almost over? They stopped again, right in front of you. The woman turned to look at the man and as she did you saw her face. You saw it and your heart gave a little leap.

For on this young woman's face, so pale and travel-weary, was a smile that made you forget taxes and Roman soldiers and even Caesar Augustus himself. In hot, noisy, crowded Bethlehem, her smile seemed to say that all the joy of heaven had come down to earth.

That night, wrapped up in your cloak on the crowded floor of your house, you could not get to sleep for thinking of her smile. It was an unusual thing, these days, to see a happy face. You wondered if the man and woman had found a place to sleep.

Why was she so happy? And you, why were you

yourself so wide-awake and excited tonight? Was it the thought of that smile that made you want to get up and dance and shout and run through the streets? You didn't do it, of course. You lay still, still as a log, so that you wouldn't wake your mother and father who were squeezed up against you on the crowded floor. But a few feet away you saw one of the other children lift his head, and you knew that he was not asleep either. None of the children who had seen Mary were asleep that night.

This was a special night. You didn't know how you knew it, but you knew that something wonderful was about to happen to you. To you and to everyone. Something so wonderful you were almost afraid to breathe for fear of breaking the stillness.

For tonight Bethlehem was very still. On other nights donkeys coughed in their stables and wolves howled from their hill tops. But on this most special of all nights, even the donkeys and the wolves were quiet. The wind itself stopped blowing. The animals and the sky and a few wide-awake children were quiet. Listening. Waiting for something.

It was very late in the night when you suddenly jumped up from the floor. In an instant the other children were on their feet. There was a commotion out in the street. You could hear men shouting, running, their sandals scuffing on the rough stones of the street. You ran to the door, stepping over sleeping grown-ups wrapped in their cloaks.

You stared at these men who were talking so loudly in the middle of the night. They looked like country men, sheepherders. What was it they were saying? They had seen an angel!

You looked at them again to make sure they were really shepherds and not lunatics. No, they were tough-looking surely, but not crazy — strong men who lived out of doors and fought wolves from their sheep with nothing but a few sticks and stones. They were not the kind of men who would be imagining things.

They had seen an angel, they repeated. And the angel had told them about a Baby born in Bethlehem and called the Baby "Savior" and "Lord." They had just seen the Baby with their own eyes — out in the stable behind the inn — and they wanted everyone else to know about it, too.

You didn't wait to hear any more. All of you children set off down the street as fast as you could run, past houses where sleepy people were stumbling to the doors, asking what all the racket was about. To the inn, then around it to the stable, then, slowly, softly, in at the door.

There she was. The young woman with the radiant

smile. She was leaning against one of the stalls, and the eyes in the happy face were closed. The man was at her side. And behind them, in the manger where the cows came for their food, was the Baby.

He was a tiny thing, wrapped tightly in a long linen band of cloth and sleeping as soundly as any newborn baby. Sleeping as though the world had not waited thousands of years for this moment. As soundly as though your life and my life and the life of everyone on earth were not wrapped up in His birth. As though from this moment on all the sin and sorrow of the world were not His problem.

Should you speak to His mother resting so quietly there? Should you ask her if you might touch the Baby — not to wake Him, but just to touch His hand?

What a moment that would have been! To have reached out your own hand and touched the Son of God!

There she was. The young
woman with the radiant smile.
He was a tiny thing...sleeping
as soundly as any newborn
baby.

And yet — do you know — I don't really envy those people, who might have been you and me. I don't envy the people who lived in Bethlehem that night, even though many of them must have seen Jesus and Mary and Joseph with their own eyes. For they couldn't have known all that they were seeing.

They couldn't know all that this Baby was born to do: the words of joy He would speak to an unhappy world, the love He would show to people too used to hatred, the victory He would win over the sin and sorrow of the world.

You and I are greatly blessed to live now, when His work of love is finished. He is as close to us today as He was to the children of Bethlehem. Closer, for today we do not even have to reach out our hands to touch Him.

If we are really sorry for our sins, we can come to Him just as truly as those shepherds did in Bethlehem. And He will forgive us and give back to us that joyous fellowship with God — lost so long ago in the Garden of Eden. This is the Christmas gift that God gives to me and to everyone on earth.

And if, on Christmas morning, when the presents are opened and the fire is burning low, we want to go back to Bethlehem, then we have only to open our

Bible to the second chapter of the Book of Luke, knowing who this man and this woman are, coming up the hill to Bethlehem. Knowing why they have come and why the angels sing. Knowing the meaning of what we read:

And while they were there, the time came for her baby to be born; and she gave birth to her first child, a son. She wrapped him in a blanket and laid him in a manger, because there was no room for them in the village inn.

That night some shepherds were in the fields outside the village, guarding their flocks of sheep. Suddenly an angel appeared among them, and the glory of the Lord shone all around them. They were badly frightened, but the angel reassured them. "Don't be afraid!" he said. "I bring you the most joyful news ever announced, and it is for everyone! The Savior — yes, the Messiah, the Lord — has been born tonight in Bethlehem! How will you recognize Him? You will find a Baby wrapped in a blanket, lying in a manger!" Suddenly, the angel was joined by a vast host of others — praising God: "Glory to God in the highest heaven," they sang, "and peace on earth, good will to all men."

BIBLE REFERENCES

Luke 2:1-12 / 18,19
Genesis 2:17 / 35
Genesis 3:1-5;10-13 / 35
Genesis 3:14 / 40
Genesis 6:5-6;14,16 / 48
Genesis 8:8-11 / 51
Genesis 12:1-3 / 58
Genesis 35:10-11 / 59
Mark 13:30-31 / 64
Hebrews 11:25 / 64
Exodus 3:10 / 65
Exodus 5:1-2 / 65
Exodus 8:8 / 67
Exodus 14:12-13 / 67,68
Isaiah 9:2,6 / 69
Micah 5:2 / 69
Luke 1:30-31 / 75
Luke 2:1-5 / 78,79
Luke 2:6-14 / 95

Christmas
Carols

Abiding in the Fields

Translation by M.E.O.

Old Welsh

Moderately slow

A-bid-ing in the fields, Were shepherds with their flocks, And on them shone a won-drous light.__ An an-gel came to them, And told this sto-ry strange, A Ho-ly Child is born this night. Oh__ bless-ing great from God, It is His Ho-ly word, And ev-er last-ing life to all.__ A faith-ful flock we'll be, And fol-low them to Thee. We haste with joy to reach Thy stall. Oh__ stall.__

All My Heart This Night Rejoices

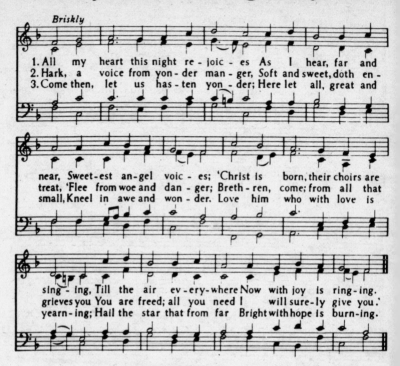

Briskly

1. All my heart this night re - joic - es As I hear, far and
2. Hark, a voice from yon - der man - ger, Soft and sweet, doth en -
3. Come then, let us has - ten yon - der; Here let all, great and

near, Sweet - est an - gel voic - es; 'Christ is born, their choirs are
treat, 'Flee from woe and dan - ger; Breth - ren, come; from all that
small, Kneel in awe and won - der. Love him who with love is

sing - ing, Till the air ev - ery - where Now with joy is ring - ing.
grieves you You are freed; all you need I will sure - ly give you.'
yearn - ing; Hail the star that from far Bright with hope is burn - ing.

The Angels and the Shepherds

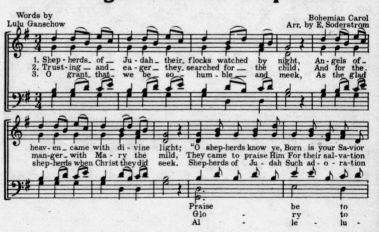

Words by
Lulu Ganschow

Bohemian Carol
Arr. by E. Soderstrom

1. Shep - herds of _ Ju - dah _ their _ flocks watched by night, An - gels of _
2. Trust - ing _ and _ ea - ger _ they _ searched for _ the child, And for the _
3. O grant that _ we be so _ hum - ble _ and meek, As the glad

heav - en _ came with di - vine light; "O shep-herds know ye, Born is your Sa - vior
man - ger with Ma - ry the mild, They came to praise Him For their sal - va - tion
shep - herds when Christ they did seek. Shep-herds of Ju - dah Such ad - o - ra - tion

Praise be to
Glo - ry to
Al - le - lu -

102

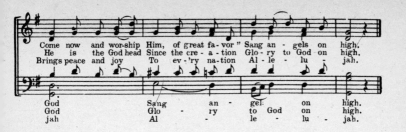

Come now and wor-ship Him, of great fa-vor" Sang an - gels on high.
He is the God head Since the cre - a - tion Glo - ry to God on high.
Brings peace and joy To ev-'ry na-tion Al - le - lu - jah.

God Sang an - gel on high.
God Glo - ry to God on high.
jah Al - le - lu - jah.

Angels, From the Realms of Glory

JAMES MONTGOMERY, 1816   HENRY SMART, 1867

1. An - gels, from the realms of glo - ry, Wing your flight o'er all the earth;
2. Shep - herds, in the fields a - bid - ing, Watch-ing o'er your flocks by night,
3. Sa - ges, leave your con - tem - pla - tions, Bright-er vi - sions beam a - far;
4. Saints be - fore the al - tar bend - ing, Watch-ing long in hope and fear,

Ye who sang cre - a - tion's sto - ry, Now pro-claim Mes - si - ah's birth:
God with man is now re - sid - ing, Yon - der shines the in - fant light;
Seek the great De - sire of na - tions, Ye have seen His na - tal star:
Sud - den - ly the Lord, de - scend - ing, In His tem - ple shall ap - pear:

Come and wor-ship, Come and wor-ship, Wor-ship Christ, the new-born King.

103

Angels We Have Heard on High

Brightly

1. An - gels we have heard on high, Sing-ing sweet-ly through the night,
2. Shep-herds, why this ju - bi - lee? Why these songs of hap - py cheer?
3. Come to Beth-le - hem and see Him whose birth the an - gels sing;
4. See him in a man-ger laid Whom the an-gels praise a-bove;

And the moun-tains in re - ply Ech - o - ing their brave de-light.
What great bright-ness did you see? What glad ti-dings did you hear?
Come, a - dore on bend-ed knee Christ, the Lord, the new-born King.
Mar - y, Jo - seph, lend your aid, While we raise our hearts in love.

Glo - - - - - ri - a in ex-cel-sis De - o, Glo - - - - - ri - a in ex-cel-sis De - o.

Auld Lang Syne

OLD SCOTCH AIR

ARR. BY
ERNEST STEVENS

Should auld ac-quaint-ance be for-got, and nev-er brought to

mind? Should auld ac-quaint-ance be for-got and days of Auld Lang

Syne? For Auld- Lang- Syne, my dear, For Auld- Lang-

Syne, We'll tak' a cup o' kindness yet, For Auld- Lang- Syne

105

Away in a Manger

Martin Luther
Arranged by M.E.O.

1. A - way in a man - ger, no crib for a bed, The
2. The cat - tle are low - ing, the poor Ba - by wakes, But
3. Be near me, Lord Je - sus, I ask Thee to stay, Close

lit - tle Lord Je - sus Laid down His sweet head; The
lit - tle Lord Je - sus no cry - ing He makes; I
by me for ev - er, and love me, I pray; Bless

stars in the sky Looked down where He lay, The
love Thee, Lord Je - sus! Look down from the sky, And
all the dear chil - dren in Thy ten - der care, And

lit - tle Lord Je - sus, A - sleep on the hay.
stay by my cra - dle, Till morn - ing is nigh.
take us to heav - en, To live with Thee there.

Bring a Torch, Jeannette, Isabella

Translation M. E. O.

Traditional Provencal
Arranged D. P.

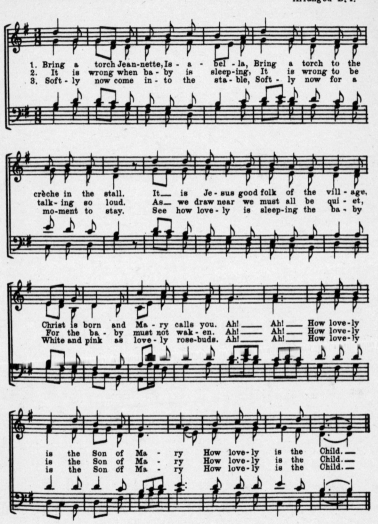

1. Bring a torch Jean-nette, Is - a - bel - la, Bring a torch to the crèche in the stall. It__ is Je - sus good folk of the vil - lage, Christ is born and Ma - ry calls you. Ah!___ Ah!___ How love-ly is the Son of Ma - ry How love-ly is the Child.___

2. It is wrong when ba - by is sleep-ing, It is wrong to be talk-ing so loud. As__ we draw near we must all be qui - et, For the ba - by must not wak - en. Ah!___ Ah!___ How love-ly is the Son of Ma - ry How love-ly is the Child.___

3. Soft - ly now come in - to the sta - ble, Soft - ly now for a mo-ment to stay. See how love-ly is sleep-ing the ba - by White and pink as love - ly rose-buds. Ah!___ Ah!___ How love-ly is the Son of Ma - ry How love-ly is the Child.___

A Child Is Born in Bethlehem

J. S. Bach

1. A Child is born in Beth - le - hem,
2. His form a sta - ble doth de - fend,

Al - le - lu - ia! And joy is in Je -
Al - le - lu - ia! Whose king - dom is with -

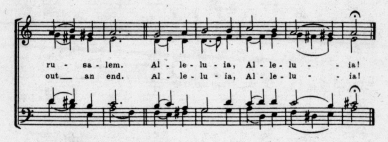

ru - sa - lem. Al - le - lu - ia, Al - le - lu - ia!
out an end. Al - le - lu - ia, Al - le - lu - ia!

3. Well did the creatures of the stall,
   Alleluia!
   Know in that Child the Lord of all.
   Alleluia!

4. There the Saba'ene Kings unfold,
   Alleluia!
   Gifts of myrrh, frankincense, and gold.
   Alleluia!

5. Exulting in that glorious birth,
   Alleluia!
   Bless we the Lord of Heav'n and earth.
   Alleluia!

6. Praise to the Holy Trinity!
   Alleluia!
   Thanksgiving unto God most high.
   Alleluia!

✱ Rests and small notes for 2nd and 6th stanzes.

Christians, Awake,
Salute the Happy Morn

Words by John Byrom

John Wainwright

Rather fast

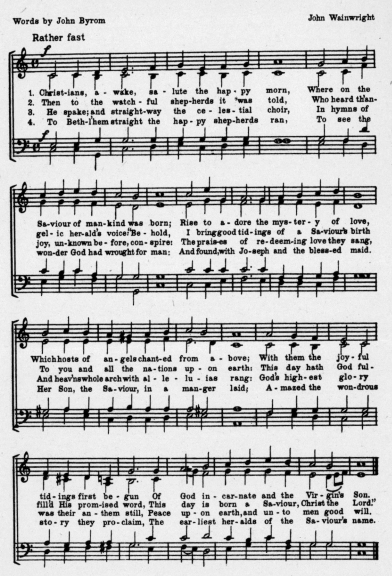

1. Christ-ians, a - wake, sa - lute the hap - py morn, Where on the
2. Then to the watch - ful shep-herds it 'was told, Who heard th'an-
3. He spake; and straight-way the ce - les - tial choir, In hymns of
4. To Beth-l'hem straight the hap - py shep-herds ran, To see the

Sa-viour of man-kind was born; Rise to a - dore the mys-ter - y of love,
gel - ic her-ald's voice: Be - hold, I bring good tid - ings of a Sa-viour's birth
joy, un-known be - fore, con - spire: The prais-es of re - deem-ing love they sang,
won-der God had wrought for man: And found, with Jo-seph and the bless-ed maid.

Which hosts of an - gels chant-ed from a - bove; With them the joy - ful
To you and all the na - tions up - on earth: This day hath God ful-
And heav'ns whole arch with al - le - lu - ias rang: God's high-est glo - ry
Her Son, the Sa - viour, in a man-ger laid; A - mazed the won-drous

tid - ings first be - gun Of God in - car - nate and the Vir - gin's Son.
fill'd His prom-ised word, This day is born a Sa-viour, Christ the Lord."
was their an - them still, Peace up - on earth, and un - to men good will.
sto - ry they pro - claim, The ear - liest her - alds of the Sa-viour's name.

Christt Was Born on Christmas Day

German

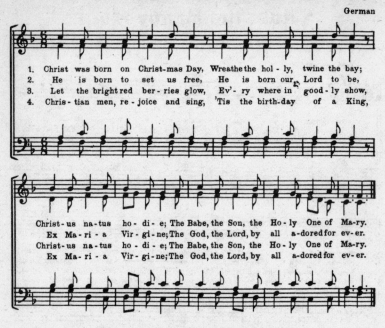

1. Christ was born on Christ-mas Day, Wreathe the hol - ly, twine the bay;
2. He is born to set us free, He is born our Lord to be,
3. Let the bright red ber - ries glow, Ev' - ry where in good - ly show,
4. Chris - tian men, re - joice and sing, 'Tis the birth-day of a King,

Christ-us na-tus ho - di - e; The Babe, the Son, the Ho - ly One of Ma-ry.
Ex Ma - ri - a Vir - gi - ne; The God, the Lord, by all a-dored for ev - er.
Christ-us na-tus ho - di - e; The Babe, the Son, the Ho - ly One of Ma-ry.
Ex Ma - ri - a Vir - gi - ne; The God, the Lord, by all a-dored for ev - er.

The Coventry Carol

"LULLY, LULLAY" From the Pageant of "The Shearmen and the Tailors"

English, 1591

Traditional Words

Arranged by M.E.O.

Slow

1. Lul - lay, Thou lit - tle ti - ny Child, By, by, lul - ly, lul - lay; ___
2. O sis - ters, too, how may we do, For to pre - serve this day; ___
3. Her - od the King, in his rag - ing, Charged he hath this day; ___
4. Then woe is me, poor Child, for Thee, And ev - er mourn and say; ___

___ Lul - lay, Thou lit - tle ti - ny Child, By, by, lul - ly, lul - lay. _
___ This poor Young-ling for whom we sing, By, by, lul - ly, lul - lay. _
___ His men of might, in his own sight, All chil-dren young, to stay. _
___ For Thy part-ing nor say nor sing, By, by, lul - ly, lul - lay. _

110

Deck the Halls
With Boughs of Holly

Words Traditional

Old Welsh

Cheerfully

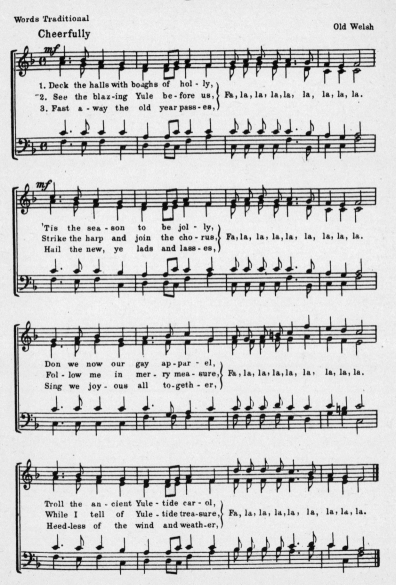

1. Deck the halls with boughs of hol - ly,
2. See the blaz-ing Yule be-fore us, } Fa, la, la, la, la, la, la, la, la, la.
3. Fast a - way the old year pass - es,

'Tis the sea - son to be jol - ly,
Strike the harp and join the cho - rus, } Fa, la, la, la, la, la, la, la, la, la.
Hail the new, ye lads and lass - es,

Don we now our gay ap - par - el,
Fol - low me in mer - ry mea - sure, } Fa , la, la, la, la, la, la, la, la, la.
Sing we joy - ous all to - geth - er,

Troll the an - cient Yule - tide car - ol,
While I tell of Yule - tide trea-sure, } Fa, la, la, la, la, la, la, la, la, la.
Heed-less of the wind and weath-er,

The First Noel

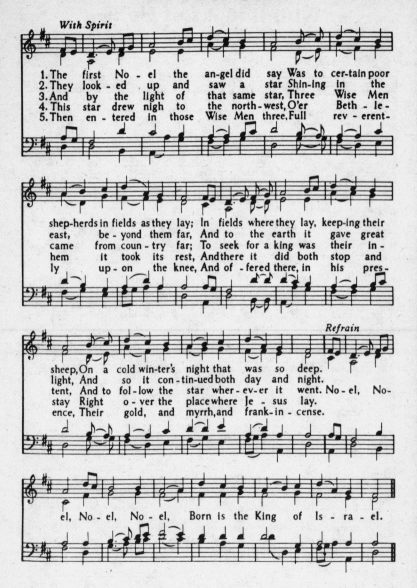

With Spirit

1. The first No - el the an-gel did say Was to cer-tain poor
2. They look - ed up and saw a star Shin-ing in the
3. And by the light of that same star, Three Wise Men
4. This star drew nigh to the north-west, O'er Beth - le-
5. Then en - tered in those Wise Men three, Full rev - erent-

shep-herds in fields as they lay; In fields where they lay, keep-ing their
east, be - yond them far, And to the earth it gave great
came from coun - try far; To seek for a king was their in-
hem it took its rest, And there it did both stop and
ly up - on the knee, And of - fered there, in his pres-

Refrain

sheep, On a cold win-ter's night that was so deep.
light, And so it con - tin-ued both day and night.
tent, And to fol - low the star wher - ev-er it went. No-el, No-
stay Right o - ver the place where Je - sus lay.
ence, Their gold, and myrrh, and frank-in - cense.

el, No - el, No - el, Born is the King of Is - ra - el.

112

From Heaven Above
to Earth I Come

Flowing

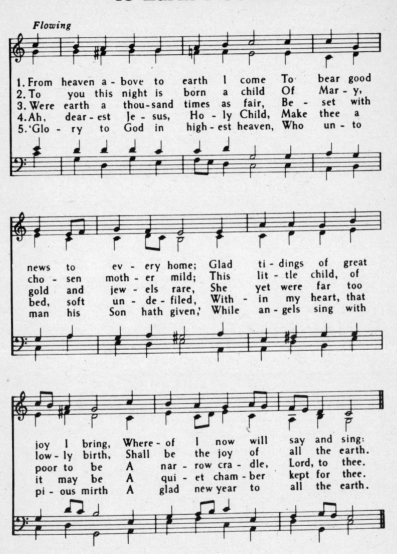

1. From heaven a - bove to earth I come To bear good
2. To   you this night is born   a   child Of   Mar - y,
3. Were earth a   thou-sand times as fair, Be - set with
4. Ah,   dear - est Je - sus, Ho - ly Child, Make thee a
5. 'Glo - ry to God in high - est heaven, Who un - to

news   to   ev - ery home; Glad   ti - dings of great
cho - sen   moth - er mild; This   lit - tle child, of
gold and   jew - els rare,   She   yet were far too
bed, soft   un - de - filed, With - in my heart, that
man his   Son hath given,' While an - gels sing with

joy I   bring, Where - of I now will   say and sing:
low - ly birth, Shall be   the joy of   all the earth.
poor to   be   A   nar - row cra - dle, Lord, to   thee.
it   may be   A   qui - et cham - ber kept for thee.
pi - ous mirth A   glad new year to   all the earth.

From Heaven High I Come to You

Luther, 1538

1. From Heaven high I come to you, To bring you tidings good and true. Good tidings of great joy I bring, To you this night is born a King.
2. This King is but a little child, His mother blessed Mary mild. His cradle is but now a stall, Yet He brings joy and peace to all.
3. Now let us all with songs of cheer, Follow the shepherds and draw near, To find this wondrous gift of Heav'n, The blessed Christ whom God hath giv'n.

Go Tell It on the Mountain

ARR. BY
ERNEST STEVENS

TRADITIONAL
CHORUS

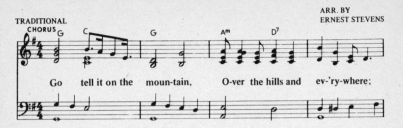

Go tell it on the moun-tain, O-ver the hills and ev-'ry-where;

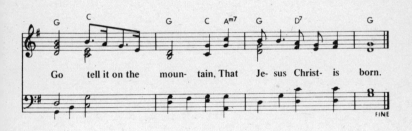

Go tell it on the moun- tain, That Je- sus Christ- is born.

FINE

VERSE

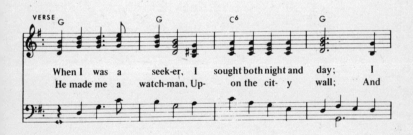

When I was a seek-er, I sought both night and day; I
He made me a watch-man, Up- on the cit- y wall; And

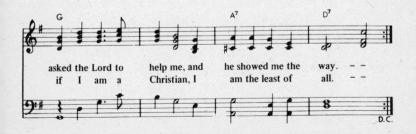

asked the Lord to help me, and he showed me the way. – –
if I am a Christian, I am the least of all. – –

D.C.

115

God Rest You Merry, Gentlemen

Traditional

Traditional English
Arranged by Sir John Stainer

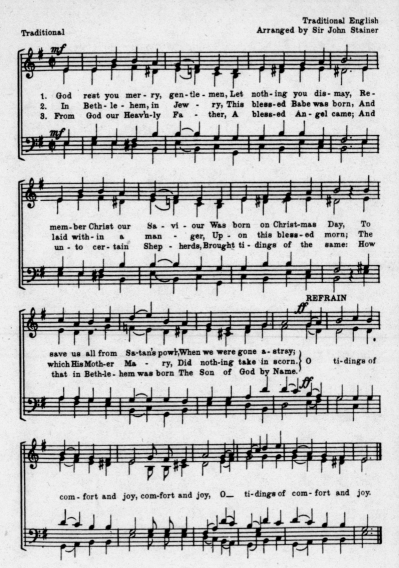

1. God rest you mer - ry, gen - tle - men, Let noth - ing you dis - may, Re -
2. In Beth - le - hem, in Jew - ry, This bless - ed Babe was born, And
3. From God our Heav'n - ly Fa - ther, A bless - ed An - gel came; And

mem - ber Christ our Sa - vi - our Was born on Christ - mas Day, To
laid with - in a man - ger, Up - on this bless - ed morn; The
un - to cer - tain Shep - herds, Brought ti - dings of the same: How

REFRAIN

save us all from Sa - tan's pow'r, When we were gone a - stray; }
which His Moth - er Ma - ry, Did noth - ing take in scorn; } O ti - dings of
that in Beth - le - hem was born The Son of God by Name. }

com - fort and joy, com - fort and joy, O ti - dings of com - fort and joy.

116

The Golden Carol

Of the Three Wise Men

Old English

Lively

1. We saw a light shine out a - far, On Christ - mas in the morn - ing, And straight we knew it was Christ's star, Bright beam-ing in the morn - ing. Then did we fall on bend - ed knee, On Christ - mas in the morn - ing, And praised the Lord, who'd let us see His glo - ry at its dawn - ing.

2. Oh! ev - er thought be of His Name, On Christ - mas in the morn - ing, Who bore for us both grief and shame, Af - flic - tions sharp-est scorn - ing. And may we die (when death shall come,) On Christ - mas in the morn - ing, And see in heav'n, our glo - rious home, That Star of Christ - mas morn - ing.

Good Christian Men, Rejoice

IN DULCI JUBILO. Irregular.

Medieval Latin Hymn
Trans. by John Mason Neale

German Melody, 14th Century

1. Good Chris - tian men, re - joice, With heart and soul and voice;
2. Good Chris - tian men, re - joice, With heart and soul and voice;
3. Good Chris - tian men, re - joice, With heart and soul and voice!

Give ye heed to what we say: Je - sus Christ is born to - day;
Now ye hear of end - less bliss; Je - sus Christ was born for this!
Now ye need not fear the grave; Je - sus Christ was born to save!

Ox and ass be - fore Him bow, And He is in the man - ger now.
He hath oped the heaven-ly door, And man is bless - ed ev - er-more.
Calls you one and calls you all To gain His ev - er - last - ing hall.

Christ is born to - day! Christ is born to - day!
Christ was born for this! Christ was born for this!
Christ was born to save! Christ was born to save!

christmas

118

Good King Wenceslas

NEALE

ENGLISH

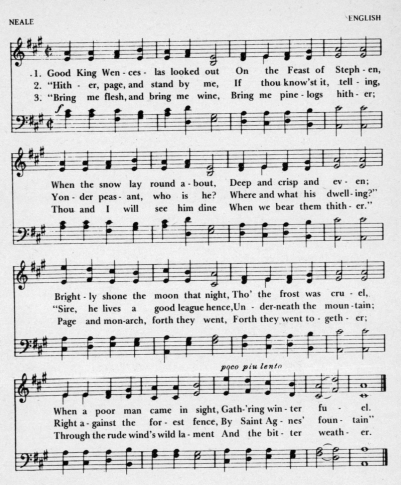

1. Good King Wen - ces - las looked out On the Feast of Steph - en,
2. "Hith - er, page, and stand by me, If thou know'st it, tell - ing,
3. "Bring me flesh, and bring me wine, Bring me pine - logs hith - er;

When the snow lay round a - bout, Deep and crisp and ev - en;
Yon - der peas - ant, who is he? Where and what his dwell - ing?"
Thou and I will see him dine When we bear them thith - er."

Bright - ly shone the moon that night, Tho' the frost was cru - el,
"Sire, he lives a good league hence, Un - der-neath the moun - tain;
Page and mon-arch, forth they went, Forth they went to - geth - er;

poco piu lento

When a poor man came in sight, Gath-'ring win - ter fu - el.
Right a - gainst the for - est fence, By Saint Ag - nes' foun - tain"
Through the rude wind's wild la - ment And the bit - ter weath - er.

4. "Sire, the night is darker now,
   And the wind blows stronger;
   Fails my heart, I know not how
   I can go no longer."
   "Mark my footsteps, my good page;
   Tread thou in them boldly:
   Thou shalt find the winter's rage
   Freeze thy blood less coldly."

5. In his master's steps he trod,
   Where the snow lay dinted;
   Heat was in the very sod
   Which the saint had printed;
   Therefore, Christian men, be sure,
   Wealth or rank possessing,
   Ye who now will bless the poor,
   Shall yourselves find blessing.

Happy Night, O Night of Splendor!

Translation by E.V. & M.E.O.

Traditional Italian

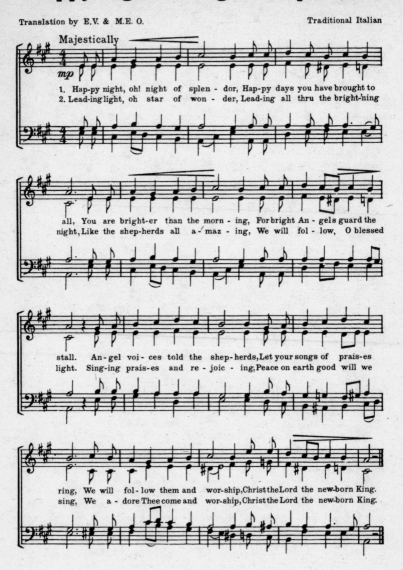

Majestically

mp

1. Hap-py night, oh! night of splen - dor, Hap-py days you have brought to
2. Lead-ing light, oh star of won - der, Lead-ing all thru the bright-'ning

all, You are bright-er than the morn - ing, For bright An - gels guard the
night, Like the shep-herds all a - maz - ing, We will fol - low, O blessed

stall. An - gel voi - ces told the shep-herds, Let your songs of prais-es
light. Sing-ing prais-es and re - joic - ing, Peace on earth good will we

ring, We will fol - low them and wor-ship, Christ the Lord the new-born King.
sing, We a - dore Thee come and wor-ship, Christ the Lord the new-born King.

Hark, the Herald Angels Sing

In moderate time

1. Hark, the her-ald an-gels sing, 'Glo-ry to the new-born King;
2. Christ, by high-est heaven a-dored, Christ, the ev-er-last-ing Lord,
3. Hail, the heaven-born Prince of Peace! Hail, the Sun of Right-eous-ness!

Peace on earth, and mer-cy mild, God and sin-ners rec-on-ciled!'
Late in time be-hold him come, Off-spring of a Vir-gin's womb.
Light and life to all he brings, Ris-en with heal-ing in his wings.

Joy-ful, all ye na-tions, rise, Join the tri-umph of the skies,
Veiled in flesh the God-head see; Hail, the in-car-nate De-i-ty,
Mild he lays his glo-ry by, Born that man no more may die,

With the an-gel-ic host pro-claim, 'Christ is born in Beth-le-hem.'
Pleased as Man with man to dwell, Je-sus, our Im-man-u-el!
Born to raise the sons of earth, Born to give them sec-ond birth.

Hark, the her-ald an-gels sing, 'Glo-ry to the new-born King!'

He Is Sleeping in a Manger

Words arranged by A. S. F. O.

Polish Carol, 16th Century
Arranged by M. E. O.

Well-marked rhythm

1. He is sleep - ing in a man - ger. chil - dren run and find Him there. Lit - tle Sa - viour, Bless - ed Je - sus, We our love do now de - clare, Come, O shep - herds, play your bag - pipes, sing your songs of joy so gay; Play sweet mu - sic here to - day, play sweet mu - sic here to - day.

2. The three Kings came from the o - rient, Bring - ing gifts of love for Him. See the love shine in their fa - ces, Love that time will nev - er dim. 'Tis the true love that each of - fers, as their hom - age they now pay; Play sweet mu - sic here to - day, play sweet mu - sic here to - day.

Here We Come A-Wassailing

ARR. BY
ERNEST STEVENS

TRADITIONAL

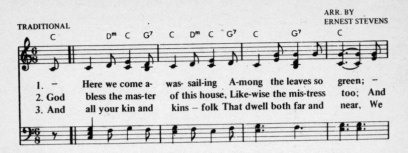

1. – Here we come a- was- sail-ing A-mong the leaves so green; –
2. God bless the mas-ter of this house, Like-wise the mis-tress too; And
3. And all your kin and kins – folk That dwell both far and near, We

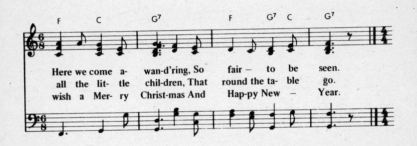

Here we come a- wan-d'ring, So fair – to be seen.
all the lit- tle chil-dren, That round the ta- ble go.
wish a Mer- ry Christ-mas And Hap-py New – Year.

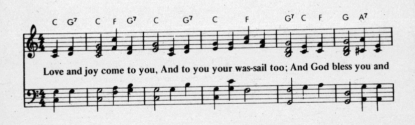

Love and joy come to you, And to you your was-sail too; And God bless you and

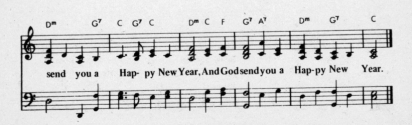

send you a Hap- py New Year, And God send you a Hap-py New Year.

I Am So Glad Each Christmas Eve

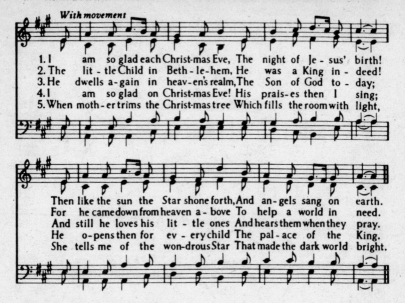

With movement

1. I am so glad each Christ-mas Eve, The night of Je - sus' birth!
2. The lit - tle Child in Beth - le - hem, He was a King in - deed!
3. He dwells a - gain in heav - en's realm, The Son of God to - day;
4. I am so glad on Christ-mas Eve! His prais - es then I sing;
5. When moth - er trims the Christ-mas tree Which fills the room with light,

Then like the sun the Star shone forth, And an - gels sang on earth.
For he came down from heaven a - bove To help a world in need.
And still he loves his lit - tle ones And hears them when they pray.
He o - pens then for ev - ery child The pal - ace of the King.
She tells me of the won-drous Star That made the dark world bright.

I Heard the Bells on Christmas Day

LONGFELLOW
CALKIN

ARR. BY
ERNEST STEVENS

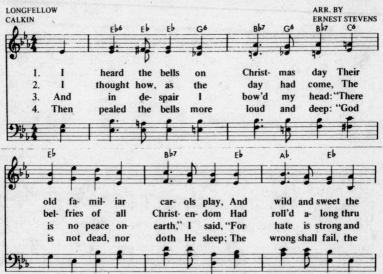

1. I heard the bells on Christ - mas day Their
2. I thought how, as the day had come, The
3. And in de - spair I bow'd my head: "There
4. Then pealed the bells more loud and deep: "God

old fa - mil - iar car - ols play, And wild and sweet the
bel - fries of all Christ - en - dom Had roll'd a - long thru
is no peace on earth," I said, "For hate is strong and
is not dead, nor doth He sleep; The wrong shall fail, the

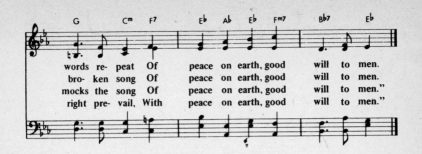

words re- peat Of peace on earth, good will to men.
bro- ken song Of peace on earth, good will to men.
mocks the song Of peace on earth, good will to men."
right pre- vail, With peace on earth, good will to men."

I Saw Three Ships

TRADITIONAL

ARR. BY
ERNEST STEVENS

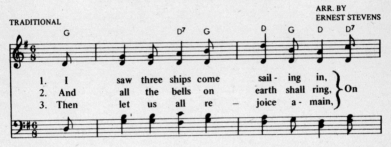

1. I   saw three ships come   sail - ing in, } On
2. And   all   the   bells   on   earth shall ring,
3. Then   let   us   all   re —   joice a - main,

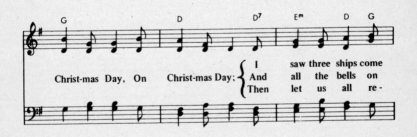

Christ-mas Day, On   Christ-mas Day; { I   saw three ships come
And   all   the bells on
Then   let   us all re -

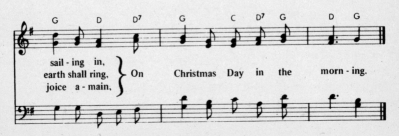

sail - ing in, } On   Christmas Day in the   morn - ing.
earth shall ring,
joice a - main,

125

In the Silence of the Night

Ancient Polish

Majestic

In the sil - ence of that night so bright, Came the

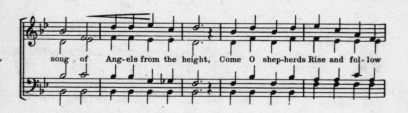

song of Ang-els from the height, Come O shep-herds Rise and fol-low

Ah!

To the stall where Je - sus lies and greet you there your Lord.

It Came Upon the Midnight Clear

With movement

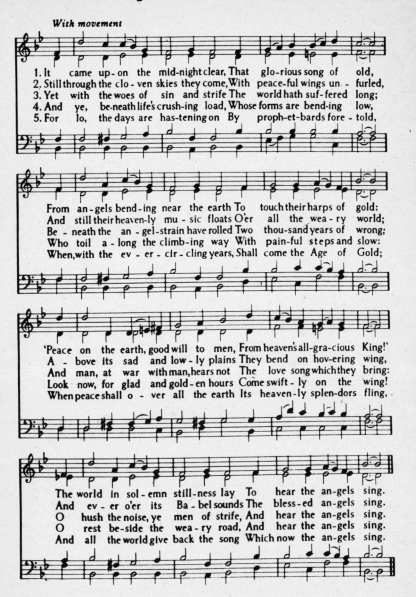

1. It came up-on the mid-night clear, That glo-rious song of old,
2. Still through the clo-ven skies they come, With peace-ful wings un - furled,
3. Yet with the woes of sin and strife The world hath suf-fered long;
4. And ye, be-neath life's crush-ing load, Whose forms are bend-ing low,
5. For lo, the days are has-tening on By proph-et-bards fore - told,

From an-gels bend-ing near the earth To touch their harps of gold:
And still their heaven-ly mu - sic floats O'er all the wea - ry world;
Be - neath the an - gel-strain have rolled Two thou-sand years of wrong;
Who toil a - long the climb-ing way With pain-ful steps and slow:
When, with the ev - er - cir - cling years, Shall come the Age of Gold;

'Peace on the earth, good will to men, From heaven's all-gra-cious King!'
A - bove its sad and low - ly plains They bend on hov-ering wing,
And man, at war with man, hears not The love song which they bring:
Look now, for glad and gold - en hours Come swift - ly on the wing!
When peace shall o - ver all the earth Its heaven-ly splen-dors fling,

The world in sol - emn still-ness lay To hear the an-gels sing.
And ev - er o'er its Ba - bel sounds The bless-ed an-gels sing.
O hush the noise, ye men of strife, And hear the an-gels sing.
O rest be-side the wea - ry road, And hear the an-gels sing.
And all the world give back the song Which now the an-gels sing.

Jingle Bells

TRADITIONAL

ARR. BY
ERNEST STEVENS

1. – Dashing through the snow, In a one-horse o - pen sleigh, –
2. A day or two a - go I – thought I'd take a ride, And

O'er the fields we go, – Laughing all the way; – Bells on bob-tail ring, –
soon Miss Fannie Bright Was seat-ed by my side; The horse was lean and lank, Mis-

Making spirits bright, – O' what fun it is to sing, A sleighing song tonight!.
fortune seem'd his lot, He got in-to a drifted bank, And then we got up-sot,

REFRAIN

Jingle bells, jingle bells, jingle all the way! Oh, what fun it is to ride in a one-horse open sleigh

Jingle bells, jingle bells, jingle all the way! Oh, what fun it is to ride in a one-horse open sleigh

128

Joy to the World

1. Joy to the world! the Lord is come: Let earth re-
2. Joy to the world! the Sav-iour reigns; Let men their
3. No more let sin and sor-row grow, Nor thorns in-
4. He rules the world with truth and grace, And makes the

ceive her King; Let ev-ery heart pre-pare Him room,
songs em-ploy; While fields and floods, rocks, hills and plains,
fest the ground; He comes to make His bless-ings flow
na-tions prove The glo-ries of His right-eous-ness,

And heaven and na-ture sing, And heaven and na-ture
Re-peat the sound-ing joy, Re-peat the sound-ing
Far as the curse is found, Far as the curse is
And won-ers of His love, And won-ers of His

sing, And heaven, and heaven and na-ture sing.
joy, Re-peat, re-peat the sound-ing joy.
found, Far as, far as the curse is found.
love, And won-ers, won-ers of His love.

129

Noël! Noël!

Traditional

French-English
Arranged by Sir John Stainer

1. 'Tis the day, the bless-ed day, On which our Lord was born, And
2. In a hum-ble feed-ing trough, With-in a low-ly shed, With

sweet-ly do the sun-beams, gild The dew-be-spang-led thorn. The
cat-tle at His in-fant feet, And shep-herds at His head, The

birds sing through the heav-ens clear, The breez-es gent-ly play, __ And
Sa-viour of this sin-ful world In in-no-cence first lay, __ And

song and sun-shine love-ly Be-gin this Ho-ly Day.
Wise-men made their off-'ring Up-on a Ho-ly Day.

REFRAIN

No-ël, No-ël, No-ël, __ No-ël, No-ël, No-ël, No-ël, __ Now

hear the sa-lu-ta-tion Of An-gel Ga-bri-el. __

130

O Christmas Tree!

O Tannenbaum!

Translated by A.S.F.O.

Traditional
German

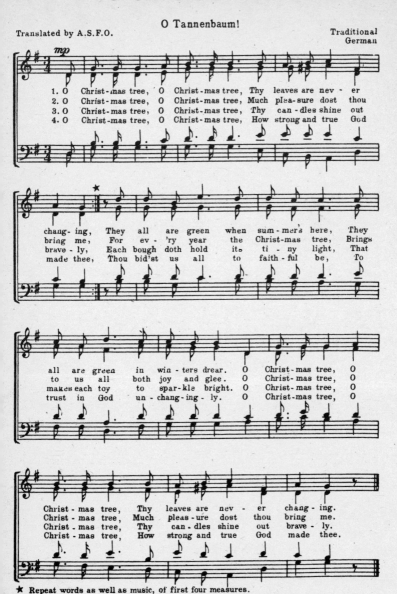

mp

1. O Christ-mas tree, O Christ-mas tree, Thy leaves are nev - er chang- ing, They all are green when sum-mer's here, They
2. O Christ-mas tree, O Christ-mas tree, Much plea-sure dost thou bring me, For ev - 'ry year the Christ-mas tree, Brings
3. O Christ-mas tree, O Christ-mas tree, Thy can - dles shine out brave - ly, Each bough doth hold its ti - ny light, That
4. O Christ-mas tree, O Christ-mas tree, How strong and true God made thee, Thou bid'st us all to faith - ful be, To

all are green in win - ters drear. O Christ-mas tree, O Christ - mas tree, Thy leaves are nev - er chang - ing.
to us all both joy and glee. O Christ-mas tree, O Christ - mas tree, Much pleas - ure dost thou bring me.
makes each toy to spar-kle bright. O Christ-mas tree, O Christ - mas tree, Thy can - dles shine out brave - ly.
trust in God un - chang-ing - ly. O Christ-mas tree, O Christ - mas tree, How strong and true God made thee.

★ Repeat words as well as music, of first four measures.

131

O Come, All Ye Christians

Translation by M. E. O.

Old Welsh

Oh come, all ye Christians, and find now God's good-ness, For He has sent to you a King. This new King has tak-en your bur-dens and sor-rows, A new life He brings to us all. His birth-place was hum-ble but Ho-ly His mis-sion, We see here the bright shin-ing stall.

O Come, All Ye Faithful

In moderate time

1. O come, all ye faith - ful, joy - ful and tri -
2. Sing, choirs of an - gels, sing in ex - ul -
3. Yea, Lord, we greet thee, born this hap - py

um - phant, O come ye, O come ye to Beth - le - hem!
ta - tion, O sing, all ye cit - i - zens of heaven a - bove!
morn - ing, O Je - sus, to thee be all glo - ry given;

Come and be - hold him, born the King of an - gels:
Glo - ry to God, all glo - ry in the high - est:
Word of the Fa - ther, now in flesh ap - pear - ing:

Refrain

O come, let us a - dore him, O come, let us a -

dore him, O come, let us a - dore him, Christ, the Lord!

O Come, Little Children

Joyously, but not too fast

J. P. A. Schulz

1. O come lit-tle chil-dren, O come one and all. The cra-dle is here as in Beth-le-hem's stall. And see what the Fa-ther, from high Heav'n a-bove, Has sent us to-night as a proof of His love.

2. O see in the cra-dle this night in the stall, See here won-drous light that is daz-zling to all. In clean love-ly white lies the Heav-en-ly Child. Not ev-en the an-gels are more sweet and mild.

3. O there He lies, chil-dren, a-sleep in the hay, While Ma-ry and Jo-seph watch Him hap-pi-ly. The shep-herds are pray-ing be-fore His rude bed, Their sweet songs are sing-ing, by an-gels they're led.

O Come, O Come, Emmanuel

VENI EMMANUEL. 8 8 8 8 8 8

Latin Hymn
Trans. by John Mason Neale

Ancient Plainsong

1. O come, O come, Em-man - u - el, And ran - som cap - tive
2. O come, Thou Rod of Jes - se, free Thine own from Sa - tan's
3. O come, Thou Day-spring, come and cheer Our spir - its by Thine
4. O come, Thou Key of Da - vid, come, And o - pen wide our

Is - ra - el, That mourns in lone - ly ex - ile here
tyr - an - ny; From depths of hell Thy peo - ple save
ad - vent here; And drive a - way the shades of night,
heaven - ly home; Make safe the way that leads on high,

Un - til the Son of God ap - pear. Re-joice! re - joice! Em-
And give them vic - tory o'er the grave. Re - joice! re - joice! Em-
And pierce the clouds and bring us light! Re - joice! re - joice! Em-
And close the path to mis - er - y. Re - joice! re - joice! Em-

man - u - el Shall come to thee, O Is - ra - el!
man - u - el Shall come to thee, O Is - ra - el!
man - u - el Shall come to thee, O Is - ra - el!
man - u - el Shall come to thee, O Is - ra - el! A-MEN.

135

O Holy Night

Adolphe Adam
Arranged by M. E. O.

136

O Holy Night *(Continued)*

sing - ing! O night— di - vine— O— night when Christ was
stran - ger! His pow'r— and glo - ry For— ev - er more pro-

born! O night— di - vine— the night our Christ was born.
bend! Be - hold— your King— be - fore him low - ly bend.
claim! His pow'r His glo - ry For ev - er more pro - claim.

137

O Little Town of Bethlehem

PHILLIPS BROOKS, 1868

LEWIS H. REDNER, 1868

1. O little town of Beth-le-hem, How still we see thee lie;
2. For Christ is born of Ma - ry; And gath-ered all a - bove,
3. How si - lent - ly, how si - lent - ly, The won-drous gift is giv'n!
4. O ho - ly Child of Beth-le-hem, De - scend to us, we pray;

A - bove thy deep and dream-less sleep The si - lent stars go by:
While mor - tals sleep, the an-gels keep Their watch of won-d'ring love.
So God im-parts to hu - man hearts The bless-ings of His heav'n.
Cast out our sin, and en - ter in, Be born in us to - day.

Yet in thy dark streets shin-eth The ev - er - last - ing Light;
O morn - ing stars, to - geth - er Pro-claim the ho - ly birth;
No ear may hear His com - ing, But in this world of sin,
We hear the Christ-mas an - gels The great glad tid - ings tell;

The hopes and fears of all the years Are met in thee to-night.
And prais - es sing to God, the King, And peace to men on earth.
Where meek souls will re - ceive Him, still The dear Christ en - ters in.
O come to us, a - bide with us, Our Lord Em - man - u - el.

Oh, Come! Shepherds

Translation by E.V. and M.E.O.

Italian

Not slow

Oh, come shep-herds come to the man-ger, Do not fear to leave your sheep; From high Heav-en an-gels now are sing-ing, And God a-bove His watch will keep Glo-ri-ous light that shines a-bove us splen-dor now glows in all the skies Light all ev-er-last-ing and en-dur-ing E-ter-nal light of Par-a-dise.

On That Most Blessed Night

Bagpiper's Carol

Translation by M.E.O.

Neapolitan
Arranged by M. E. O.

With swaying motion

On that most bless-ed night When Je-sus Christ was

The two lower voices humming

born So bright-ly shone the star a-bove 'twas ra-diant as the

morn The an-gels sing-ing, Their voic-es ring-ing O-ver

Beth-le-hem so fair There hung a love-ly star____ Its

beam-ing rays shone forth a-far, to guide the wise men there.

The Perfect Rose

Translation by A.S.F.O.

Danish
Arranged by M.E.O.

1. Our ros - es bloom and fade a - way, Our in - fant
2. Oh! lit - tle world re - joice and sing, Let glad - some
3. Christ walks for - ev - er by our side, His love shall

Lord __ a - bide al - way. May we __ be bless-ed His
tid - ings ev - er ring. The rose __ of heav - en has
all __ our wants pro - vide. A low - ly rose __ He

face to see And ev - er lit - tle chil - dren be.
come to earth, God's glo - ry brought in Je - sus birth.
blos - soms fair, And gives to all __ His ten - der care.

A Shepherd Band
Their Flocks Are Keeping

Praetorius, 1609

Slow

1. A shep-herd band their flocks are keep-ing, And
   gen-tle lambs are sweet-ly sleep-ing. When sud-den-ly they all be-
   hold An an-gel in bright robes with harp of gold.

2. Glad ti-dings of great joy he bring-eth, The
   a-zure vault with an-thems ring-eth. Im-man-u-el a-wakes the
   song And count-less hosts the glor-ious theme pro-long.

3. The shep-herds view the host re-turn-ing, Their
   hearts with ho-ly ar-dor burn-ing. To Beth-le-hem they wend their
   way Re-peat-ing with glad tongues th'an-gel-ic lay.

Shepherds Hurried to Bethlehem

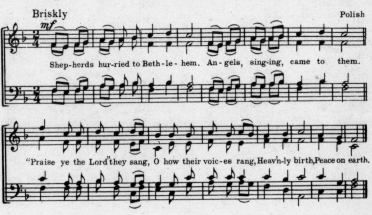

Polish

Briskly

Shep-herds hur-ried to Beth-le-hem. An-gels, sing-ing, came to them.
"Praise ye the Lord" they sang, O how their voic-es rang, Heav'n-ly birth, Peace on earth.

142

Shepherds!
Shake Off Your Drowsy Sleep

Besançon
Arranged by Sir John Stainer

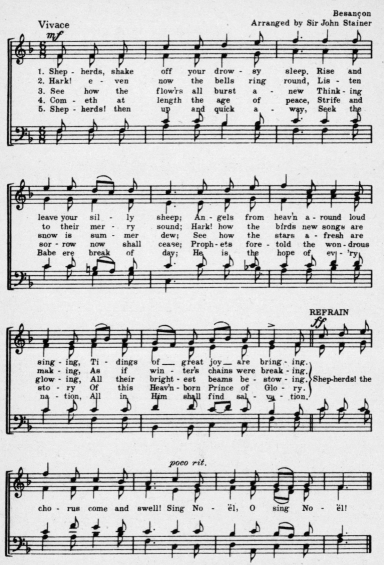

Vivace — *mf*

1. Shep - herds, shake off your drow - sy sleep, Rise and
2. Hark! e - ven now the bells ring round, Lis - ten
3. See how the flow'rs all burst a - new Think - ing
4. Com - eth at length the age of peace, Strife and
5. Shep - herds! then up and quick a - way, Seek the

leave your sil - ly sheep; An - gels from heav'n a - round loud
to their mer - ry sound; Hark! how the birds new songs are
snow is sum - mer dew; See how the stars a - fresh are
sor - row now shall cease; Proph - ets fore - told the won - drous
Babe ere break of day; He is the hope of ev' - 'ry

REFRAIN *ff*

sing - ing, Ti - dings of __ great joy __ are bring - ing.
mak - ing, As if win - ter's chains were break - ing.
glow - ing, All their bright - est beams be - stow - ing. } Shep-herds! the
sto - ry Of this Heav'n - born Prince of Glo - ry.
na - tion, All in Him shall find sal - va - tion.

poco rit.

cho - rus come and swell! Sing No - ël, O sing No - ël!

Silent Night

Franz Grüber
Harmonized by Sir John Stainer

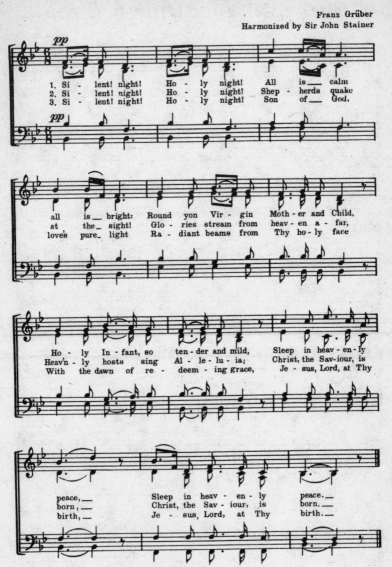

1. Si - lent! night! Ho - ly night! All is calm all is bright: Round yon Vir - gin Moth - er and Child, Ho - ly In - fant, so ten - der and mild, Sleep in heav - en - ly peace, Sleep in heav - en - ly peace.

2. Si - lent! night! Ho - ly night! Shep - herds quake at the sight! Glo - ries stream from heav - en a - far, Heav'n - ly hosts sing Al - le - lu - ia; Christ, the Sav - iour, is born, Christ, the Sav - iour, is born.

3. Si - lent! night! Ho - ly night! Son of God, love's pure light Ra - diant beams from Thy ho - ly face With the dawn of re - deem - ing grace, Je - sus, Lord, at Thy birth, Je - sus, Lord, at Thy birth.

Sleep, Holy Babe!

Rev. E. Caswall

John B. Dykes

1. Sleep, Ho-ly Babe! up-on Thy moth-er's breast; Great Lord of earth, and sea, and sky, How sweet it is to see Thee lie In such a place of rest, In such a place of rest.

2. Sleep, Ho-ly Babe! Thine An-gels watch a-round, All bend-ing low with fold-ed wings, Be-fore th'in-car-nate King of kings, In rev-'rent awe pro-found, In rev-'rent awe pro-found.

Thou Didst Leave Thy Throne

MARGARET. Irregular. Ref.

Emily E. S. Elliott

Timothy R. Matthews

1. Thou didst leave Thy throne and Thy king-ly crown When Thou
2. Heav-en's arch-es rang when the an-gels sang, Pro-
3. Thou cam-est, O Lord, with the liv-ing Word That should
4. When the heav-ens shall ring, and the an-gels sing, At Thy

cam-est to earth for me; But in Beth-le-hem's home
claim-ing Thy roy-al de-gree; But in low-ly birth
set Thy peo-ple free; But with mock-ing scorn,
com-ing to vic-to-ry, Let Thy voice call me home,

was there found no room For Thy ho-ly na-tiv-i-ty:
didst Thou come to earth, And in great hu-mil-i-ty:
and with crown of thorn, They bore Thee to Cal-va-ry:
say-ing, "Yet there is room, There is room at My side for thee:"

REFRAIN

1-3. O come to my heart, Lord Je-sus! There is room in my heart for Thee.
4. My heart shall re-joice, Lord Je-sus! When Thou comest and call-est for me. A-MEN.

CHRISTMAS

146

The Three Kings

Traditional

Flemish Carol
Arranged by M. E. O.

1. Late, three wise Kings a - far off did go. A - jour - ney - ing thro' the keen frost and deep snow. All through the land, Joy - ful - ly came, For Je - sus they sought then en - thrall'd by His fame. Drums sound - ed their march as they quick - ly drew near. Drums sound - ed their march as they quick - ly drew near.

2. Thus to Saint Joseph an an - gel did say "To E - gypt now speed thee, nor fear to o - bey. Her - od comes nigh, Ven - geance to reap" Fast jour - ney'd the ass while Ma - ry did weep. So Jo - seph did com - fort the maid in her tears. So Jo - seph did com - fort the maid in her tears.

3. Came the dread word that lit - tle ones all Should straight be cut off or tak - en in thrall. What ear hath heard, What heart can tell, Aught of the fear of some deeds that be - fell Such ten - der lambs robb'd of dear life at a word. Such ten - der lambs robb'd of dear life at a word.

147

The Twelve Days of Christmas

OLD ENGLISH

ARR. BY
ERNEST STEVENS

1. On the first day of Christmas, my true love gave to me a par-tridge in a pear

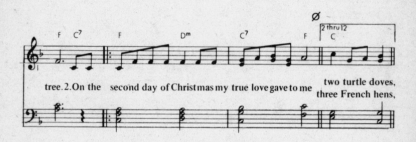

tree. 2. On the second day of Christmas my true love gave to me two turtle doves,
three French hens,

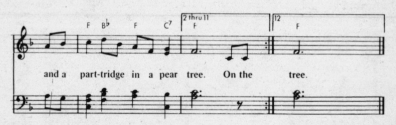

and a part-tridge in a pear tree. On the tree.

3. three French hens
4. four mocking birds
5. five gold rings
6. six geese a-laying
7. seven swans a swimming
8. eight maids a milking
9. nine drum-mers drum-ing
10. ten piper's pip-ing
11. eleven ladies danc-ing
12. twelve lords a leap-ing

Ø REPEAT THIS PART, EACH
TIME ADDING ONE PART

There's a Song in the Air

CHRISTMAS SONG. 6 6 6 6 12 12

Josiah G. Holland

Karl P. Harrington

1. There's a song in the air! There's a star in the sky!
2. There's a tu-mult of joy O'er the won-der-ful birth,
3. In the light of that star Lie the a-ges im-pearled,
4. We re-joice in the light, And we ech-o the song

There's a mo-ther's deep prayer, And a ba-by's low cry!
For the Vir-gin's sweet boy Is the Lord of the earth.
And that song from a-far Has swept o-ver the world.
That comes down through the night From the heav-en-ly throng.

And the star rains its fire while the beau-ti-ful sing,
Ay! the star rains its fire while the beau-ti-ful sing,
Ev-ery heart is a-flame, and the beau-ti-ful sing,
Ay! we shout to the love-ly e-van-gel they bring,

For the man-ger of Beth-le-hem cra-dles a King!
For the man-ger of Beth-le-hem cra-dles a King!
In the homes of the na-tions that Je-sus is King!
And we greet in His cra-dle our Sav-iour and King! A-MEN.

149

We Three Kings of Orient Are

J. H. Hopkins, 1857

Tutti. 1. We three kings of O-ri-ent are;
Melchior. 2. Born a King on Beth-le-hem's plain,
Caspar. 3. Frank-in-cense to of-fer have I,
Balthazar. 4. Myrrh is mine, its bit-ter per-fume
Tutti. 5. Glo-rious now be-hold Him a-rise,

Bear-ing gifts we tra-verse a-far, Field and foun-tain, moor and
Gold I bring, to crown Him a-gain, King for-ev-er, ceas-ing
In-cense owns a De-i-ty nigh, Pray'r and prais-ing, all men
Breathes a life of gath-er-ing gloom; Sor-rowing, sigh-ing, bleed-ing,
King and God and Sac-ri-fice, Al-le-lu-ia, Al-le-

moun-tain, Fol-low-ing yon-der star.
nev-er, O-ver us all to reign.
rais-ing, Wor-ship Him, God most High.
dy-ing, Seal'd in the stone-cold tomb.
lu-ia; Earth to heav'n re-plies.

REFRAIN
a tempo

O— Star of won-der,

star of night, Star with roy-al beau-ty bright, West-ward

lead-ing, still pro-ceed-ing, Guide us to Thy per-fect light.

150

We Wish You a Merry Christmas

ARR. BY
ERNEST STEVENS

TRADITIONAL

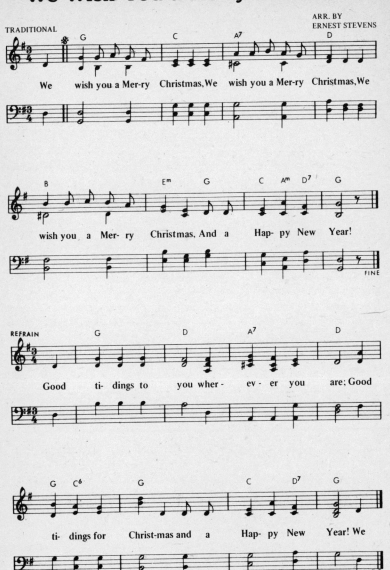

We wish you a Mer-ry Christmas, We wish you a Mer-ry Christmas, We

wish you a Mer-ry Christmas, And a Hap-py New Year!

FINE

REFRAIN

Good ti-dings to you wher-ev-er you are; Good

ti-dings for Christ-mas and a Hap-py New Year! We

D.S.

151

What Child Is This?

DIX

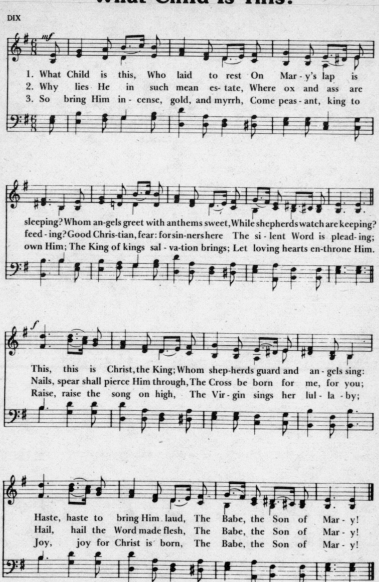

1. What Child is this, Who laid to rest On Mar - y's lap is
2. Why lies He in such mean es- tate, Where ox and ass are
3. So bring Him in - cense, gold, and myrrh, Come peas - ant, king to

sleeping? Whom an-gels greet with anthems sweet, While shepherds watch are keeping?
feed - ing? Good Chris-tian, fear: for sin-ners here The si - lent Word is plead-ing;
own Him; The King of kings sal - va-tion brings; Let loving hearts en-throne Him.

This, this is Christ, the King; Whom shep-herds guard and an - gels sing:
Nails, spear shall pierce Him through, The Cross be born for me, for you;
Raise, raise the song on high, The Vir - gin sings her lul - la - by;

Haste, haste to bring Him laud, The Babe, the Son of Mar - y!
Hail, hail the Word made flesh, The Babe, the Son of Mar - y!
Joy, joy for Christ is born, The Babe, the Son of Mar - y!

When Christmas Morn Is Dawning

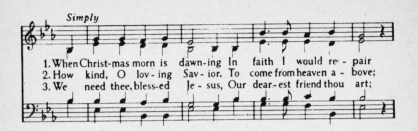

1. When Christ-mas morn is dawn-ing In faith I would re - pair
2. How kind, O lov-ing Sav-ior, To come from heaven a - bove;
3. We need thee, bless-ed Je - sus, Our dear-est friend thou art;

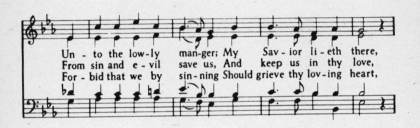

Un - to the low-ly man-ger; My Sav-ior li-eth there,
From sin and e - vil save us, And keep us in thy love,
For - bid that we by sin-ning Should grieve thy lov-ing heart,

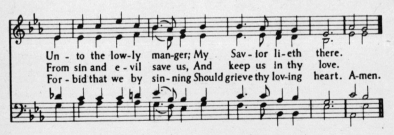

Un - to the low-ly man-ger; My Sav-ior li-eth there.
From sin and e - vil save us, And keep us in thy love.
For - bid that we by sin-ning Should grieve thy lov-ing heart. A-men.

While by My Sheep I Watched at Night

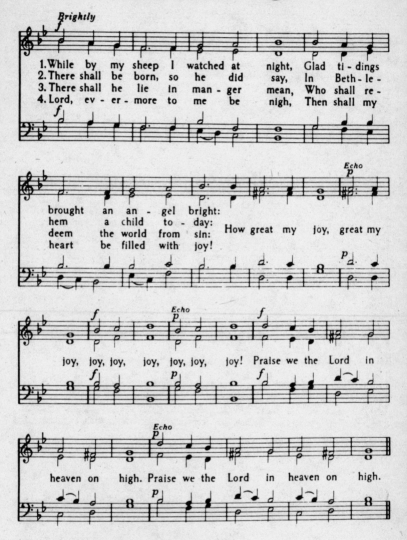

1. While by my sheep I watched at night, Glad ti-dings
2. There shall be born, so he did say, In Beth-le-
3. There shall he lie in man-ger mean, Who shall re-
4. Lord, ev-er-more to me be nigh, Then shall my

brought an an-gel bright:
hem a child to-day: How great my joy, great my
deem the world from sin:
heart be filled with joy!

joy, joy, joy, joy, joy, joy, joy! Praise we the Lord in

heaven on high. Praise we the Lord in heaven on high.

A few voices may be selected to sing the "Echo" parts.
Harmonization copyright 1960, Augsburg Publishing House.

154

While Shepherds Watched Their Flocks

Traditional

Melody from Thomas Este's
"Whole Book of Psalms", 1592

1. While shep - herds watched their flocks by night, All
2. "Fear not," said he, for might - y dread Had

seat - ed on the ground, The an - gel of the
seized their trou - bled mind. "Glad ti - dings of great

Lord came down, And glo - ry shone a - round.
joy I bring To you and all man - kind."

3. "To you in David's town this day
   Is born of David's line
   The Saviour who is Christ, the Lord,
   And this shall be the sign.

4. "The heav'nly babe you there shall find
   To human view displayed;
   All meanly wrapped in swathing bands,
   And in a manger laid."

5. Thus spoke the Seraph, and forthwith
   Appeared a shining throng
   Of angels praising God, who thus
   Addressed their joyful song.

6. "All glory be to God on high,
   And to the earth be peace;
   Good will hence forth from heav'n to men,
   Begin and never cease."

While Shepherds Watched Their Flocks

CHRISTMAS. C.M.

Nahum Tate

George F. Handel, arr.

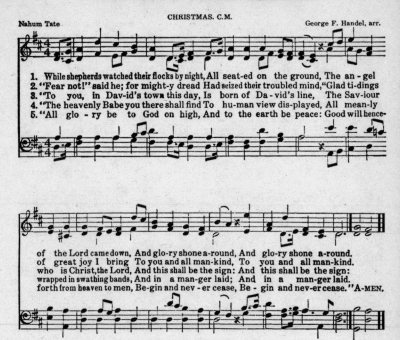

1. While shepherds watched their flocks by night, All seat-ed on the ground, The an - gel
2. "Fear not!" said he; for might-y dread Had seized their troubled mind, "Glad ti-dings
3. "To you, in Dav-id's town this day, Is born of Da-vid's line, The Sav-iour
4. "The heavenly Babe you there shall find To hu-man view dis-played, All mean-ly
5. "All glo - ry be to God on high, And to the earth be peace: Good will hence-

of the Lord came down, And glo-ry shone a-round, And glo-ry shone a-round.
of great joy I bring To you and all man-kind, To you and all man-kind.
who is Christ, the Lord, And this shall be the sign: And this shall be the sign:
wrapped in swathing bands, And in a man-ger laid; And in a man-ger laid.
forth from heaven to men, Be-gin and nev - er cease, Be - gin and nev-er cease." A-MEN.

156

You Came Down From Heaven

Translation by M.E.O.

Early Italian

Rather slow

You came down from Heav'n to low-ly birth, God of love brings joy to earth. You a pil-grim from the star-ry sky, Now man's form to glo-ri-fy. Oh! my Je-sus, Sweet-est babe Di-vine, Oh! hold for-ev-er__ our love in Thine. Oh! my Je-sus, Oh! my Je-sus, Hold for-ev-er our love in Thine.

157

Index